I0741852

STWAS
The Second Book

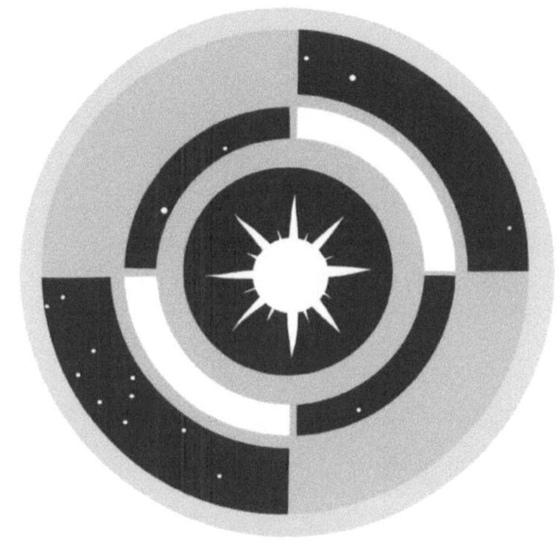

LISA SAMSON
LEN SWEET

The Salish Sea Press
Orcas Island, Washington

St.As
The Second Book

Paperback ISBN: 978-1-63613-019-4
eBook ISBN: 978-1-63613-020-0

First published in the United States December 2021, by The Salish Sea Press, a division of SpiritVenture Ministries, Box 1493, Absecon, NJ 08201.

Artwork and illustrations by Lisa Samson: lisasamson@gmail.com

Interior design by Carmen Barber: keepingyouwriting@gmail.com

Acknowledgements

Many thanks to Carmen Barber whose tireless efforts and positive attitude makes our work that much more joyful.

Thank you to all at SpiritVenture, to our families, friends, colleagues, fellow creatives, and all who have supported us over the years.

We couldn't do this without you.

Dedication

To Dede Hutcheson
and the Windgate Foundation:

With gratitude and appreciation
for your belief in this project.

I did not believe in vain.

Chapter One

Small Camels, Large Hearts

Once upon a time, Zebby the Noble Camel held his long neck aloft like the prow of a ship. His regal face, like a figurehead, looked with favor upon the waves of sand over which he had traversed many miles in his lifetime. In the days of King Herod and Caesar Augustus, he wore silks and tassels dyed in shades of jeweled treasure, and he bounded across the desert with magi. Magi were priests from Mesopotamia, the same area from which Father Abraham (we'll get to him shortly) originally hailed. They were peculiar servants of The Most High God. Most of God's servants are. Trust me on this. Magi had been around for quite some time by then. They read the skies, and when something of note arose in another land—some call it an omen, others a portent, perhaps you might recognize the word *sign*—they saw it as their duty to let the ruler of that kingdom know.

Now Zebby the Noble Camel stood one head and a quarter of a neck shorter than all the other camels where he lived. He zipped with the smooth speed of a horse, was as wise as a donkey, and saw himself freer than any bird that ever flew. And do you know why? Zebby was loved by the human he helped.

This makes all the difference. It's how The Creator

designed it, though humans tend to lord their place in creation over the rest of us. If you don't like hearing that, imagine how we beasts of burden feel *living* it! We have feelings too, you know.

Zebby's human was named Caspar. Although a few gray hairs had begun to collect about his ears, Caspar was known by some as a mage, by others as a sage, but all could agree he possessed more wisdom than age. This phenomenon sometimes occurs when foolish parents are given a wise child. And such was the case with the cheeky and charming Caspar.

Caspar and Zebby never left home without a sack of dried dates, Zebby's favorite treat, hanging from Caspar's belt. Caspar dressed in beautiful robes. Caspar wore red boots. Zebby loved those boots. And not only did Zebby love those boots, he *knew* he loved those boots. And he knew *why* too. Even from afar, Zebby always recognized Caspar.

If having the best human on the planet wasn't enough, Zebby had what all humans adore: an interesting story.

Though unable to tell his own illustrious and beats-all tale to the humans, Zebby nevertheless held that knowledge inside of him like a secret honor bestowed by a most just ruler. But I heard it one night not long ago, and so I, Issy the Donkey, share it with you now.

Like many good stories, this one starts well before the beginning with a famed ancestor, in this case, Kizzy the Little Camel. Think of it as two stories for the price of one, a bargain at any bazaar, market, or hearthstone. I do what I can.

Before he was ever named, this camel grazed the grounds surrounding Jerusalem (Salem at the time) and he belonged to Melchizedek, the Priest-King of Salem. The camel, however noble his future offspring claimed, was simply left behind one day by a resting caravan and Melchizedek felt sorry for him. He was smaller than all the other camels and nobody really thought him much good for anything other than being a bit of a curiosity.

One day, Father Abraham (Abram in those days) showed up in Salem to pay tribute to Melchizedek after he had committed a great act of valor. You see, some kings had attacked the city of Sodom where his nephew Lot lived. They took anything worth taking, including some people, including Lot. (Lot definitely hadn't been put on this earth to make life easier for his uncle. Just ask anybody who knows.)

Abram wasn't having any of that. No, siree. He already had three hundred and eighteen battle-trained people of his own as well as a couple of good friends who added themselves to the posse. They chased those kings down, pursuing them over hill and through valley. And they prevailed. The offending kings returned the spoils of the city of Sodom, including some people, including Lot, who, not surprisingly and in case you were wondering, still went on to make life more difficult for his uncle. In other words, your difficult relatives might not be that strange after all.

The King of Sodom met Abram when he showed up at Melchizedek's to give El Elyon, The Most High God, a tenth of what had been returned. Minus the people, including Lot.

Melchizedek met them with bread and wine and blessed Abram with these words:

> "Blessed be Abram by God Most High,
>   Creator of heaven and earth.
> And praise be to God Most High,
>   who delivered your enemies into your hand."

After Melchizedek received the offering, The King of Sodom told Abram, "Keep the rest of the city's returned spoils."

Abram refused. "I don't want you to take credit for anything that I do from here on out," he said. Abram was beholden to no one, you see. He trusted that God would be faithful. And that faith? It was his righteousness! Not deeds he had done, nor the grand thoughts he might have had in his mind, but his faith in The Most High. Faith in God makes anything possible. Jot that down.

Seeing the opportunity as ripe, considering Abram already owned a host of camels and what difference would one more truly make, Melchizedek brought "that little camel" to Abram. It wasn't really fanciful or a great display of honor and show.

"I have no need of this camel. My work is right here where I am," Melchizedek said to Abram. He sighed and adjusted his headpiece. "I'm here. I'm always here it seems. Humans being what they are and all."

"These twin hills *are* beautiful, though," said Abram looking around him.

"A holy place, indeed. But no reason for this camel at this point. I'm sure you see what I mean."

Abram squinted. "Oh, you're *giving* me this little camel?"

"Yes. If you're willing to take him."

"Sure. No problem."

As this interchange was passed down through the ages, more and more embellishment attached itself, lots of bowing and such, as to render it almost unrecognizable. Nevertheless, we don't need to go there. It would just cement the misconception that God doesn't speak with us as we are, that we must get fancy with our dialogue to impress The Most High. We can't fool El Elyon, though.

Much of the time God starts with the humble, the mundane, the everyday, as the seed from which extraordinary things grow. Jot that one down, too.

"Were you born in these parts?" Abram asked Melchizedek.

"In a manner of speaking." The Priest-King leaned forward. "This place will see great, mighty, and terrible things. And the greatest love the world will have ever known."

Now Abram had no need for a little camel at that distinct point in time either, but like many things given us directly by The Most High, the time might come. So he kept his mouth shut because, although a great patriarch with trained men and many servants, he was learning the same lessons most humans must, including how to receive gifts from God. Abram bowed and offered his thanks.

Another mouth to feed, he thought, then thought again, for then as now, some humans realize that God works in ways we cannot know ahead of time or even understand in the very present. *All in good time, Abram*, he said to himself. *You never know.*

Melchizedek, a holy man who heard the voice of God Most High and delivered messages to the people of the land, a king who served bread and wine, patted the camel's back. "You know more than you let on, don't you?"

The little camel barely noticed Melchizedek for the only thing special about him at the time was his size, remarkable in the way all small things are, through no fault of their own, and yet we love them because of it. God made them thus and isn't that wonderful?

Abram shrugged and took hold of the camel's harness.

As the group wandered away, Melchizedek raised his hands to the sides of his mouth and called out, "Name him Kizzy! That will give me a laugh for a good long time!"

And that is how he got his name.

Abram raised a hand and slowly the caravan wandered away from the vicinity of the twin hills and its loving Priest-King and highly-esteemed friend of The Most High God, Melchizedek. (If you would like to know, The Most High esteems all friends of God most highly. Even donkeys. I would most *definitely* jot that down if I were you.)

As Abram began his journey home, The King of Sodom collected the city's belongings, including the people, and not including Lot, and went his way. When Abram ventured beyond Salem's boundary, he turned and looked back. Melchizedek stood on the hill, arms outstretched, receiving the morning sun. The hill reminded Abram of a skull.

I've seen it many times, myself. It always makes me shudder a little.

And so Father Kizzy, the illustrious patriarch of Zebby's line, did what he was told by Father Abraham, and walked his not-so-great, round feet where he was led. He carried a boy named Isaac when the family picked up their tents to find more grazing places for their flocks. He carried Isaac's mother Sarah. In fact, he was the perfect choice for bearing smaller humans to places they needed to go.

Kizzy never saw Melchizedek again and didn't think of the Priest-King in his white robes and his palace in Salem. He forgot Melchizedek's wife and the household servants who made delicious food and bread and wine and offered a place of rest to weary travelers. He simply led a camel's life, becoming a "ship of the desert" as his type were called.

And he drank a lot of water.

That part about camels is absolutely true, as you know.

One day, when Father Abraham was nearing the end of his life, he worried about what would happen to his son and heir, Isaac. Isaac, though not a young man anymore, remained without a wife and children. This was of great concern to his father who wanted to make sure the family would continue and so receive The Most High's promise that they would be numbered like the stars of the sky and the sands upon the shore.

Kizzy the Little Camel had learned a camel song passed down through the ages:

Sand and stars innumerable.
Life is uncountable.
This even the camel knows.
Even the camel knows.

Father Abraham sent his most trusted, senior servant to the lands of his birth to find a wife for Isaac among his native people. The servant, (we don't know his name) wanted to make sure he located the right woman. So he set up a rather elaborate scenario for The Most High to follow. The Most High doesn't always agree to these things, just so you know. But on that day . . .

The servant drew into town with ten camels, including Father Kizzy, loaded with gifts for the mysterious bride to be. "Let the one who offers to give me water, and to all of my camels as well, be she who has been chosen for my lord's son, Isaac," he whispered, his words picked up by the hot wind through which they had traveled.

Water for ten camels?

Ladies and gentlemen, do the math. Fill the cistern of your mind with the realization that this is more water than you give your cat. Perhaps in its lifetime. And let it also be recognized the servant's bargain was suited to his own benefit at the expense of another. Humans ask for that sort of thing a lot.

Nevertheless, The Most High let him get away with it. That time.

They all stood around the well for a moment as the servant considered whether or not it had been a good idea to constrain The Most High with such specificity, when a young woman strode up to the well with her water jar expertly balanced on her shoulder. Though formed beautifully at the work bench of The Creator, she nevertheless appeared to be no stranger to daily toil. The light brown skin of her forearms shone with perspiration as the sun kissed them in their work. She drew water into the jar and the servant knew that she would most likely be back to the well several times before moving onto her next chore.

Even better than all that: she sang! As she pulled the bucket up, her muscles contracted as she emptied the water into the jar. This she did several times and the servant enjoyed her song.

He and his camel train drew right up to the well.

The young woman stood straight and looked him in the eye. "Well, look at you," she said, swiping her hands together. "And coming with all of those camels, too. Long trip?"

"Yes, it was."

"I'll bet you're thirsty." She dried her hands on her tunic. "Would you like some water?"

"I'd be grateful."

The young woman grabbed the dipper that sat by the well, filled it from her jar and brought it to the servant who drank it all.

"Another?"

He nodded, handing back the dipper. "Thank you."

He held his breath.

She submerged the bowl of the dipper into the jar once more. "It's easy to get thirsty out here, isn't it? And your camels? Shall I draw water for them too? Of course I shall! Nobody with a sound mind would refuse an offer like that." She laughed, the sound as pleasing as her song.

Some people are nothing *but* song, the servant thought, unable to believe that his request had been granted, yet clearly unable not to see what was going on right in front of him. That's the way it is with The Most High.

"Of course," she continued with a laugh, "nobody with a sound mind would even offer."

"You said that, not me," he joined in with a smile. "But I am grateful. More grateful than you can know."

She busied herself drawing jar after jar, her face dripping with sweat, swiping it away between trips with her forearm. And somehow, it only served to make her more lovely. Yes, this was definitely the woman for Isaac, the servant realized. You see, the servant had known Isaac from birth. And though Abraham's son was now forty years old, he wasn't any less deserving of this woman. In fact, he was a peaceful, prosperous man, given to the life his father had set down for him, a man of trust and goodness. Yes, this woman would be a wonderful partner.

The Most High knows, he thought, and thought again.

Well, Kizzy and the others drank and drank and drank.

And drank and drank and drank.

And drank.

Oh, why not?

And drank some more!

Kizzy fell in love with the young woman. Camels do so at the drop of a hat, a cloak, a bracelet, or a wineskin. They try to hide it behind a very contrary personality. And a lot of spitting.

Just when the servant thought they clearly had enough, she pulled yet more from the well and deposited it in the troughs for those to come.

She guided the servant and his train to her home, and not surprisingly, she was indeed a relative of Father Abraham. Her name was Rebecca.

That's a beautiful name, Kizzy thought.

See that right there?

Kizzy *thought*. And not only did Kizzy think, he clearly had an opinion. And not only did Kizzy have an opinion, he *knew* he had an opinion.

And the little camel said to himself right then and there, *If I do nothing else for my offspring, I will pass on to them the power to watch, to wait, and finally, to know. And to know that they know.*

For *thinking* you know when you don't is a sneaky lie of its very own kind.

This he did. Father Kizzy passed down the secret of knowing to his favored offspring, a she-camel named Ramah, who passed it down to her favored one, and so on. What constituted a favored one? Well, that is the camels' secret and humans aren't allowed in on how they assess each other, or even *if* they actually do.

But let it be known, all the favored ones were just as small as their ancestor. You see, if the large, the mighty, the smart, and the well-to-do are favored, that is nothing new. But the small, the oppressed, the ones deemed weak, the ones who maintain their calling despite an obvious disadvantage—well, favoring them is a very good thing. The Most High does it all the time. I would definitely jot that down if I were you.

Kizzy continued to grow in wisdom and truth as he plied the trade of supporting the humans who assumed camels into their service. He observed the world on many trails and through many trials: winds and biting sandstorms, days where water was nowhere to be found, loads too heavy to be borne in comfort, the weight bearing down on his bones, hard boots that kicked him without a thought.

The line of thoughtful camels migrated over the years, almost two thousand years, from the lands of Father Abraham all the way to the place where the sun rises upon the Parthians. It finally settled down within the walls of a magnificent, noble man with priestly duties who counted stars and raised his eyes to the glories of the heavens for signs and wonders.

Yep. Caspar. And Kizzy's little relative, long down the line, Zebby, raised his great brown eyes to the heavens too. He listened. He knew a messiah was coming. He knew, after all he had seen, the world needed this desperately.

Now you know too.

No need to jot that down.

Welcoming the news is all that is required. The rest it will accomplish on its own, in you, through you, and for you. This, even the camel knows.

And donkeys, too.

We did not search in vain.

Chapter Two

Zebby wasn't just small, he was fast, with feet "more sure than water being wet or fire being hot." That's what Casper told him. Zebby accompanied the star-searching priest on many trips into the desert, the wilderness, and the mountains to view the sky. Casper carefully rendered the position of the stars on parchment.

Wearing silken threads and tassels, Zebby stood by Caspar as he took out the prophecies of old, readying himself for the possibility of the great star appearing. "The one that says a king of kings, a god among men, will be born!" Casper said on every trip as if speaking it would make it so.

Each year for two decades, Zebby and the priest zoomed to the four points of the earth and back again. Together they watched above the horizon for the new and promised light.

"Zebby," Casper said as they sat together before the dancing campfire, the wise man leaning against the camel's side, "these are my favorite times of the year. You and me, nobody else. Thank you, my noble friend."

Noble Friend. Zebby wished everybody knew his real title!

He loved their travels, came to hope, too, in this Promised One Casper spoke of with such life, for the world was a solemn place at times, violent at others, and people, like camels, carried a weight that seemed to drag them down, first and foremost from within. Perhaps this star, this light in which Caspar hoped and dreamed, would meet the wise man's expectations. Maybe it would even change the world.

And maybe Zebby's world too, for not all camels were as loved as Zebby and Zebby knew it! If Caspar looked forward to something, he would do the same.

One day, on a journey home from a council of stargazing priests who followed prophecies and noticed signs, a time they compared notes and divined what to do next, Casper gripped the reigns and sought to control his breath.

"It has come," he whispered to Zebby and as to Earth herself. "The Light has come in the east."

Caspar pointed into the depths of the sky. "See there?"

Zebby did! It shone with such clarity, such beauty!

And suddenly Caspar knew what he had told Zebby was now a hope fulfilled. "The Light has come!" he cried. "The Light has come!" He raised his hands toward the heavens. "The Light has come!"

He dropped to his knees and wept.

All the years of looking, hoping, wondering, despairing, and looking again, and again, and again, hadn't been for nothing. They had all led him right to that place, to that very moment where a belief became knowing.

Finally, he gained his feet once more. Ready. "I have to make calculations, of course, but I'm relatively sure all the signs point to the land of Israel."

Zebby had never been there. He had heard they much preferred donkeys. (Which is absolutely true.)

"Let's get back home, my friend."

Zebby knelt while the priest settled into his saddle.

As Zebby rose, he let out the customary grunt camels emit when inconvenienced. And let me tell you, getting to your feet with a human being straddled over your spine is not as easy as it looks!

Caspar laughed. Zebby grumbled, but tossed his tassels.

Well, Zebby had never run as quickly as he did that night. Over the purple hills sleeping beneath the starlight, they hurried back to Caspar's palace.

Caspar gathered his charts, summoning his servants with a loud voice. "Load the camels, pack my clothes, provisions-provisions-provisions!" He clapped his hands. "You know what to do, everybody! Let's get the others!"

There wasn't a person in the palace that didn't know who the others were—Balthazzar, a scholar, and Melchior, a prince, both priests. In those days, priests weren't paid for being priests. They were born into it and supported their daily lives like everyone else does, by work or inheritance. Preferably by inheritance. Some things never change.

Like Caspar, they were committed to the prophecies, committed to searching the stars for the great star's arrival. What joy there would be in the telling of the good news. And not just the good news, the *great* news!

The people who dwelled in darkness have seen a great light! And light dispels darkness. Every single time. Jot that one down, for sure.

It wasn't long before they set out.

They first found wise and fragile Balthazzar, for he was very old. Next they located the regal, quick-witted Melchior, younger than the others, stronger, and a touch too passionate about his feelings and opinions for humans to relax completely in his presence. Caspar, to use the new lingo on the trade routes told him frequently to, "Rein it in, your royal highness."

That night however, they stood looking up in silence, years of faith come to knowledge. And if the star appeared, so would the One whose birth it proclaimed. There could not be one without the other.

"We will welcome the Light born into the world together," said old Balthazzar. "I have one last journey in me, brothers." They clasped hands and ate a great feast to commemorate their fortuitous existence. "To be born at such a time," Melchior said, raising his hands, "is a great honor."

"We travel to the west. The land of the setting sun and The Promised One!" Caspar declared.

Balthazzar cleared his throat. "We overtook that land not that very long ago, brothers. And we would have kept it had it not been for Rome. We might meet some trouble. Herod will want to know why we are there."

Herod, the king of Israel, was a despotic ruler, prone to illness and madness, and he loved a good show. Three Parthian priests telling tales of a new king born in *his* land? Now there was something to be concerned about.

Melchior pointed to the old man. "Well said. So we need to make sure Herod knows we aren't there to take over the land of Israel."

"With this huge entourage you always travel with, Melchior? We'll need a firm plan." Balthazzar lifted his turban and ran a hand over his bald head.

"We don't need a plan. We'll just tell him the truth," said Caspar.

Balthazzar almost wept. "That we've come to *worship* this *new* king? Oh, that sounds much better."

Caspar squeezed the old man's shoulder. "Fear not, friend. The Most High is with us."

A week later, the camel-and-donkey train was loaded up with yet more supplies and gifts the three wise ones had gathered, shuffling, tense, and ready to depart. Zebby awaited, head high at the front, his the first step, his the first motion at the click of Casper's tongue.

There. The signal.

The journey had begun.

I did not
hope in
vain.

Chapter Three

Simeon's Promise

Years before the magi set out, the Holy Spirit spoke to a man named Simeon when he awakened in his home on a chilly morning in the land of Israel. Hearing his wife's soft breathing, Simeon drew the covers more closely in, tucking the bottom of them under his feet. His knuckles brushed the underside of his beard and he opened his eyes to a new day. The sun, rising in the east, had not yet crested the earth, but the red sky was ripe for the coming of the news.

"You will not die before you see the Lord's Messiah, light of the Gentiles, and the glory of the Jews, come to save in the presence of all humanity."

"Lord?" Simeon whispered to the audible voice surrounding him, no lips visible in the room save those of his sleeping wife. He sat up.

"You will not die before you see the Lord's Messiah, light of the Gentiles, and the glory of the Jews, come to save in the presence of all humanity."

The voice, neither deep nor trilling, resonant like a valley, higher than the mountains, held love, expansion, patience, and yes, confidence. Complete assurance? That too. And Simeon believed not only God had spoken, but that, yes—"I have heard . . . the Lord!"

Simeon was a young man, pleased to serve, ready to see in front of him at any time what his heart clung to in faith.

The hope of this world is coming, and in my lifetime!

To Jew and Gentile alike. "To all the people!" he cried. "All of them! All of us!"

Simeon jumped up from their bed, threw the covers off his nakedness, raised his arms and praised The Living God. Simeon would bless himself with that memory over and over in a time when Jerusalem was under siege by the Parthians. He would bless himself with the memory when Herod took over, cruelty like a black cloud around the Idumean monarch, and all was not well in the land of Israel.

That day, he fell to his knees and wept.

Jehovah-Ezer had not forgotten the promises given to Israel.

The Deliverer was coming.

I did not keep going in vain.

Chapter Four

The Deliverer Has Come!

The town of Bethlehem slept for the second time that night. Bowls were cleaned and stacked, the washing done, the morning readied for. In the houses where people lived, ate, fed their animals and their children, Bethlehemites had banked their fires, turned down their covers, extinguished the flames of their oil lamps, said their prayers, and climbed into their beds. Darkness settled in until the sun would rise again. And it always does, friend. I have seen it more thousands of times than any human, believe me. I look great for being fourteen hundred years old, because this I know: the sun always rises again.

Animals rustled in the stables, night bugs scritched and buzzed, and breezes from the mountains moved grass effortlessly. It traveled down the narrow lanes, skirted rooftops, and dropped in on those who chose to sleep there. In some houses, mothers hushed their infants and fed them back to sleep, praying the other children wouldn't awaken. In others, people prayed the unbearable staccato of a family member's snore would stop long enough for them to find slumber.

Bethlehem slept much like any city or town unaware of what is to come, settled in the peacefulness of stillness, even though heartache would meet them.

No stone would remain unturned, no one truly untouched by the decision one madman can make when he is sick and dying in body, mind clouded, and spirit unattended to. That man was Herod. Called Herod the Great. Although to many people's minds Herod the Horrible would have better suited the harsh reign and personal temperament of this king of Israel. Please be it known he was a political king, installed by the good graces of the Roman Empire. No child of Abraham had any say in the matter.

Bethlehem slept as I looked out upon her from the window of my stable where I was living with my family: Joseph, Mary, and their young child, Jesus. Bethlehem slept right next door, or down the street, or the next street over to their Messiah, The Promised One, the One who loved them more than anyone ever had, save, as Jesus would come to call The Creator, Our Father. I had been here, right in this stable, when Mary birthed Jesus into the world.

And what a night it was!

Shepherds, angels, heavenly light, a star, family, love unbounded, and me, Issy the donkey. Formerly known as Balaam's Ass, I'm a faithful servant of The Most High and the bearer of The Messiah. My centuries on the trade routes gave me the name Starlight. I've been in wars, storms, and stretches of desert where I wondered if I would die from lack of water. I've been beaten, overloaded, and disregarded entirely.

And I have been loved.

Intensely and beautifully loved.

By Mary, then by Joe when he came into our lives.

And now, Jesus loves me, too.

This I know. And when you *really* know, you know that you know.

When he grins, the light of heaven already in his eyes flares up and envelops us.

When he eats his food with the happiness that good flavors give to humans, it's all the rest of us can do not to laugh. And don't get a donkey laughing! Our hee-haws can be quite disconcerting.

Not that Jesus ever minds.

I can't help but feel Jesus loved us before we ever loved him.

Jesus slept, too. Cradled in the crook of his mother's arm, who, in turn, was held in the arms of Joe. The stars shone.

Bethlehem slept. Sleep city of David. Sleep while you dream yourself to be in safety.

And I will dream along with you.

I turned from the stable window and walked to the gate that separated the human living quarters from the animal living quarters. In the winter, we beasts are a wonderful source of heat, if I do say so myself! All that breathing. All that blood flowing.

All is quiet inside my family's place.

I turn toward the red heifer in her stall in the back corner.

Now I know, and you can know because you've decided to read my tale, that this red heifer was without spot or blemish. She was a perfect sacrifice to be made for the land of Israel. Not that she had been called upon to do so. She just could have.

"You're up early, Issy" she said in Bovine.

Thankfully, I speak Bovine.

"Yes. I'm feeling something is stirring. Something important."

Donkeys have a very keen sense of danger. Poor horses. They can be easily convinced. Not so the donkey! If you want to endanger yourself, we won't stop you. But we do draw the line if you want us to go barreling off the edge of a cliff! You can do that just as well by yourself, thank you very much.

The red heifer said, "Just imagine how scared you would be if you were perfect like me."

"You're very beautiful, Heffy," I said, knowing that what she was frightened of was also a source of pride. I would give that to her. Heffy lived a very quiet and solitary life. "But I'm talking about something in the air. The way the winds blow. They are breathing change. Can you smell it the way I do?"

Heffy breathed in deeply through her great, round nostrils. "Hmm. Perhaps." She breathed in again. "Is it that aroma that is at once musky and also clear like ice?"

"You're smelling it."

"Oh. Well, if change is coming perhaps we should prepare!"

I wanted to ask how, but trust me when I say heifers do not like to be put on the spot.

"Perhaps we should. But some changes come as they will and all we can do is respond. It feels like that kind of change. Anyway, I know one of the best things to do before any day is to get a good night's sleep."

She nodded, trying to look like a sage. "Goodnight, then, Issy."

"Goodnight, beautiful friend."

Now by the gate, I folded my legs beneath me, ready to awaken, already ready for Joe to load his masonry tools into my baskets, and very much ready to head with him to the job site.

Jesus, ten months past his first birthday, lifted his head. "Issy!"

"Shh. Shh," whispered Mary into his curls, and fell back asleep.

Mary was with child again. She was very tired.

Jesus grabbed his mother's face and kissed it, right on her nose, and settled back in.

I turned to Heffy. "You have nothing to worry about, Heffy. You won't be the one heading to Jerusalem to die."

How do I know these things? Ask The Most High.

I did not trust in vain.

Chapter Five

A Just Man

The first tale I told you was about me and Mary. This one is about me and Joe. Joe's important. He was put on this earth to father Jesus and so he has. Joe came from a family full of goodness and graciousness. They understood that the law without the love was a bunch of hee-haws in a very dry and thirsty land. And yet, they were devoted to it in their own behavior, following it in a manner that most people in Israel failed to.

Joe knew the law. He had studied Torah and the oral law, too. Spoken word was important to Joe's family. Perhaps it was because of his utter truthfulness and honesty, not to mention his humility, for Joe was just, fair, kind, and good, which attracted him to The Most High, to raise Jesus with Mary. I may be a smart donkey, but things like this, well, I guess at, just like you do. For who can know the innermost thoughts of the mind of God? The secret council of the One Infinite Creator?

Joe surprised me that morning. I hadn't heard him stir. My night had been filled with dreams of children crying and women screaming, men shouting, and there was blood. His touch atop my head, his fingers scratching into my mane, his soothing, husky voice, pulled me from the night.

"Good morning, girl," he said, having taken to calling me that since we moved to Bethlehem. Yep, I was Joe's girl, Mary's friend, and Jesus's playmate. That baby loved for me to sit down so he could crawl all over me and slide down off my back into the straw. His laughter! Now, if I was a human, I would say it was better than wine for the effect it had.

I gave a soft squeak.

"You ready for another day?"

I rose to my feet and nodded my head. A great big dip.

"I swear you know what I'm saying."

Little did he know I not only knew what he was saying, I could answer back if I so chose. An angel gave me the gift of speech a long time ago, and there are no take-backs with God. Only hand-backs on our part.

Joe ran his rough, stone-mason's hand along my neck, down over my shoulder, up over my withers, and down my back as I drank from the trough. And then, because Joe is Joe, he scratched me on the forelock, then in-between my ears. Oh, and ah. Joe, you are a good, good man! Because let me tell you, here in Israel there are people that keep the law because they're scared not to and those who keep the law because they want to follow God, to get close to God, to experience God's tender mercies and everlasting love.

I'll bet you know which kind of man Joe is!

I ate some food as he cleaned his tools. The day before had been extra long.

Joe smiled at me as he settled my baskets. "Well, girl, let's get you loaded up."

Mary walked into the stable, Jesus following her at a run. "Issy!" he cried, just like the night before.

Mary rubbed the small of her back. Her pregnancy had started to show two months previously. "Now, Joe. Be careful today."

Joe laughed. "Oh, my carefree love, you are one to talk!"

She held a hand to her mouth and laughed with a nod. "I just don't know what we'd do without you. Don't forget your food. Jesus and I will get it ready." She held out a hand to her son.

He pointed to me. "Issy. Ride Issy!"

Joe knelt down. "She's got to work with me today, Son."

Jesus stomped his foot. "Abi, I would like to ride Issy."

"I know, Son."

Get used to disappointment, I thought.

His eyes lit up. "Tonight! Ride Issy tonight."

"Jesus . . ." Joe said.

"Ride Issy tonight?" Jesus asked, looking up at his father through his lashes.

"Well said, Son. You may ride Issy tonight. Ask and you shall receive."

Jesus laughed and ran into the house.

"You're too soft with him!" cried Mary.

"Perhaps. But I can't help but think the world is going to toughen him up like it does the rest of us."

"Hopefully not in the same way." Mary handed him a sack holding bread, olives, and figs.

"Definitely not. But he will be a man of sorrows, my love. Acquainted with grief. I don't want to add to them."

"But a man of great love, nonetheless." Mary's words held in them a firmness that truth enables. For truth is never hard like a club. Its firmness is somehow able to be sculpted to fit into the ear of the listener without breaking its drum. For what good does deafness do when we are made to listen to and sing along with the Eternal Song? This song is founded in The Creator's everlasting, unchanging, healing, restoring love. "And you"—she put her arms around his neck, her belly between them—"are the right man to help teach him that."

"Well, I sure do love you two."

"And many other people as well."

Joe's face reddened a touch. He bent his head and gave his beloved wife a kiss.

The Messiah had come, everybody! And already he was filled with love and the need to experience everything he could. No, the world wouldn't toughen him into someone calloused and hard. I couldn't imagine it. Not with those eyes.

But he *would* know compassion. He would suffer with us; he would know. He would *know*.

And isn't that at the very heart of The Most High?

We did not
gather in vain.

Chapter Six

We covered the three-and-a-half-mile road to Jerusalem in an hour, the same trek we had been making since the family decided to stay in Bethlehem. Mary's family hadn't taken kindly to her pregnancy. It was too risky to return to her hometown.

Joe was helping to finish The Temple that Herod, yes, the same mad king aforementioned, had greatly expanded. At least he was smart enough to know that coming between an Israelite and their God was grounds for an even more difficult reign.

We walked through the main temple gate, a Roman eagle centered over the top. Carved in stone.

Man might carve things in stone, but God made the stone to begin with. Jot that down.

The people of Jerusalem hated that eagle. They called it an abomination. For Rome to set its seal upon The Temple of the Lord, honoring the Emperor and his claim to deity? Well, this donkey doesn't even begin to understand that kind of delusion. I can't speak for us all.

Joe settled me in a spot of shade with some other donkeys, gathered his carving tools, and made his way to the area where other stone carvers worked in the Court of the Gentiles.

Come closer and let me tell you something you might not know. Jewish people don't just live in Israel. They are scattered all across the Roman Empire, as well as Egypt, and they made converts of the people Jews call the Gentiles. People who weren't born into Jewish families but came to believe in the God of Israel came to Jerusalem for festivals too. It was a sight to see when people from many nations were gathered. However, because they weren't born into Jewish families, they had to stay in the outer court.

When we came home that night, Joe spoke with his father about such humans. "Abi, I don't know about all that anymore. I have had some conversations with Gentiles about our God, and they know Adonai. They truly do. I'm coming to the point where I don't understand the difference anymore."

"They're not circumcised, Son. They're unclean."

Joe nodded. "Yes, I know." Then shook his head. "It's simply the more I get to know them, the harder it is to understand why Adonai would think less of them for the families they were born into."

"We didn't write the law. We just keep it."

Joe picked up Jesus. "I wonder what he'll think about it when he grows up?"

Jesus pointed at me. "Issy!" he cried. "Time for ride, Abi?"

Mary stood up from where she had placed my food in the manger. "He doesn't forget *anything*." She rolled her eyes.

Everyone laughed.

"I can take him out if you want," Mary offered.

Joe was tired. Work at the temple had been going on for years, but as Herod's health declined, the pace felt more demanding. I had to give the madman credit for I have seen a lot of magnificent buildings over the years, created by the greatest architects of humanity. Yes, I'm speaking of the pyramids. I'm speaking of Babylon. Of Greece and Rome. Of Cathay. And Herod the Great was great because he was a builder, a man who created massive structures, who literally moved mountains, whose dreams were large in scale and wide in scope. He was a man whose will demanded it should be so, would be so, and finally was, indeed, so.

But he couldn't have done any of that without donkeys. Humanity rose upon our backs, friend. It surely did. You can thank me later after you're done reading this story.

"Let's go together," Joe suggested. "I could benefit from walking the hills."

Mary made sure I had my fill of the fresh water drawn from the Wells of David and Jesus sat on me while I drank. "Issy, drink!"

And soon enough, we were watching the sun set and night begin to fall over the land. We walked slowly, Jesus now quiet.

"You know," said Mary. "I grew up around a lot of Gentiles, traders, and those traveling up and down the highway. Mother used to reprimand me for talking to them, but I couldn't help myself. I always wanted to know things about the world."

"I liked that about Nazareth."

"Of course, with Sepphoris a few miles away, too, a goodly portion of it Gentile, well, that made for interesting talk around the evening meal."

Jesus patted me. "Gentile!"

His parents laughed.

He was right, you know. I began my history with a prophet from Moab. They're the descendants of Esau, by the way. But Jesus loved me. And I don't think there was an "anyway" about it.

He laid his upper body along my neck and I felt a certain light flare up inside of me when his chest rested on me. The light had come. Indeed, it was so.

"Speaking of Gentiles," Joe said, "Jerusalem was troubled today, my love."

"How so?"

"Apparently, Parthians came from the east. They had quite a company with them. Though nobody knows why yet."

"Oh, dear."

There wasn't an older person near Jerusalem that didn't remember Parthia's siege on the city fifty years before. And their families had heard all the tales. Those were bleak times. Thankfully at that time, my family—for I had been with them for many years—were from the land of Syria. Those were desperate times in Israel. All the land knew about it.

"They went directly to Herod. So now it's anybody's guess what's really going on. Their people are encamped near the city."

"How many?"

"Two hundred or so?"

Those Parthians travel in style, let me tell you. I could only imagine how their camels looked. They like to decorate them. They like to decorate a lot of things. But don't mistake artistry for gentleness. I have watched them battle and it isn't something I ever need to see again. They are fierce and they are excellent warriors.

He went on. "All Jerusalem is troubled."

"Hopefully you'll find out tomorrow why they've come."

Jesus patted my neck. "Ride, Issy!"

Joe smiled, took my rope and Mary's hand. "Tomorrow will tell us of itself, then. Let's enjoy the evening, my love."

"Love," Jesus said, and laid his head on me.

We did not learn in vain.

Chapter Seven

Stargazers

When we arrived home, the stars were fully bloomed and the moonlight pooled its reflected glory on anything unobstructed. It shone through the windows of the stable and through the front door of the house even as a light breeze cooled the space.

And it shone on two people who weren't there when we had set out. Mary rushed over to the table where her brother Levi and her cousin Simon stood to their feet.

She pulled Levi into her fierce embrace. "Oh! Oh, Levi! Look at you!"

And then her cousin. "Simon, Simon! You came!"

"Let me get Issy put up," said Joe from the doorway. "You two are a welcomed sight."

He led me in, past Heffy, and to the manger to resume my meal.

"Who are those people?" she asked.

"Relatives." I took a mouthful and chewed. "Levi used to be a very strict mess. And Simon was the opposite. A very loose mess. But their love for Mary has seen them in good stead. And now Jesus. Well, that baby keeps them coming back for visits despite her brother Joachim still being angry at her for getting pregnant in the first place."

"Still? How long humans hold grudges!"

"I wish it was only a grudge. He wants to kill her!" I nodded. "Joachim has the others trapped. They don't want to kick him out, he is a hard worker, and they're worried that he will harm Mary if she and Joe return to Nazareth."

"Well, Bethlehem is better anyway." The cow raised her nose.

I squeaked in agreement. "There isn't too much good that comes out of Nazareth, as they say."

Actually, the true saying is, "Nothing good comes out of Nazareth," but that simply isn't true. If it ever really was, mind you. God doesn't abandon anyone or any place. Good is always around for those with eyes to see it, ears to hear it, tongues to taste it, noses to . . . well, you get the idea, don't you?

Joe's mother, Ruth, set out the daily bread that had not yet been consumed, some olive oil, cheese, and mixed herbs. A great bowl of lentil stew joined the rest on the wooden table. "We waited for you to get back, Son, and a good thing, that! This is just the way I like an evening meal. Good people, good food, and catching up on all the doings elsewhere." Her eyes glittered like Joe's did when love was in the room.

They sat on the benches, Mary gathering Jesus onto her lap, who immediately got down and put his arms up to Uncle Levi. "Up, Levi?"

Levi laughed. "How can you not do what he asks?" He lifted him onto his lap.

"That face gets you every time," said Simon, turning to Mary and Joe. "I felt an urging to come, and Levi did too. What's going on?"

Winds of change, my friend. Obviously they smelled them like we did.

Joe's face twisted into confusion. "Things seem to be going just fine. Mary?"

"Oh yes! Look how Jesus is growing, and speaking now, too."

Levi shrugged. "I just felt a ripple in my spirit."

"Me too." Simon reached for the bread, tore off a piece worth several bites, and dipped it into the oil.

Joe dug a piece of bread into the stew, scraping off the excess against the side of the bowl. "There was some news today in Jerusalem. I'm actually surprised you didn't hear it coming through."

"Oh, the magi?"

Joe raised his brow. "Is that what you heard? I thought they were Parthians."

"They are," said Simon. "Oh!" He took a small sack from his belt. "Here,

Ruth. Some salt mined in the Himalayas. For you. We stopped at a spice merchant."

Ruth took it. "Now this will make our stews even better. Thank you both."

"So they're probably not going to siege the city," Joe said.

Levi settled a hand on his nephew's shoulder. "I doubt it. There is a nice entourage, but not enough to keep Jerusalem from being Jerusalem."

Now let me tell you a little something they *don't* know. Don't think they're stupid. They just didn't spend hundreds of years on the trade routes like I did.

Priests, particularly those who serve El Elyon, or as I like to call God, The Most High, take it upon themselves to deliver messages when they are given one. They get them in various ways, but one of them is by observing the heavens—star-gazing—and believing that nothing happens by accident and the heavens will tell of it in advance. A lot of people don't like this sort of thing, but I'm just reporting who they are. Better to simply rely on The Most High, day by day, I have found.

However, these priests did it in service to humanity, not to gather wealth or power over others. Do with it what you will. We donkeys ask far less complicated questions. We know whatever *it* is, God will make of it something good. No matter how fallen it seems right now. No matter how much we fail to understand.

And I have found to be true that The Most High looks upon the heart. If you jot anything down, jot that.

Once upon a time, long ago, however, there lived a man who came to be known as Alexander the Great. He literally wanted to take over the world. Granted, the world in his mind was quite a bit smaller than it actually is, but we will allow him his ignorance in the face of what really is, that is not yet known. Donkeys tend to know what we don't know.

Supremely self-indulgent, over three hundred years ago he was of a mind to take over Babylon. No shocker there. A group of magi approached him with a warning saying, "If you enter Babylon, you will meet your end."

And they were right.

Do with that as you will, too. They were right a lot of the time. And all truth comes from The Most High. Jot that down, too.

The wise men were not Parthian warriors. I could have told them that very day. But years ago, though I am able to speak—just ask Balaam the prophet—I chose never to do so again until I would meet The Messiah. My family would just have to figure this out for themselves.

Now what these magi had come to tell Herod? That was the true mystery. May it be good news.

I did not consent in vain.

Mary's Heart for Home

"How's my mother?" Mary asked after the old people, babies, and most of us in the stable had bedded down for the night. Of course, Old Is's ears are always perked and ready to hear. "And Joachim?"

Ugh. Joachim. I've forgiven him, but I can't bring myself to like him, yet. Not while he's still frothing at the mouth over something that happened so long ago, something that availed us all of this wonderful baby boy. Let it go, Joachim. Let. It. Go.

Simon leaned forward. "Joachim is in love."

"Oh?" Mary's lips curled up. A bit. "Has it—"

"Softened him?" interrupted Levi. "A little."

"Mother must be thrilled."

The two men laughed. Levi tapped the table with his fingertips. "She knows Joachim as well as any of us do. She feels sorry for Rachel."

I didn't even know Rachel and already I was on her side. We jennies need to stick together.

"Still, perhaps someday soon." Mary looked at her hands laid flat. I knew her heart, you see. And she missed her family sorely.

Levi cleared his throat. "In any case, your home is being cared for well by Simon and myself. I think now might be a good time to approach the family. You can't run from Joachim forever." He leaned forward on his forearm. "People are getting tired of his angry complaining. I don't think you'll have to worry about the people of Nazareth. They've listened to him for so long even they're tired of the way they have felt."

"Who wants to have *that* in common with anyone?" Simon, ever willing to enjoy his life, said.

Joe put his arm around Mary. "Maybe we can go home soon. Issy and I can head up there and see the lay of the land for ourselves."

Oh, yes. Me and lays of the land go hand in hand. Or hoof in hoof, I should say.

Mary's face brightened in a spot I didn't even realize had been in shadow, and I thought I knew every inch of it. "Oh, would you, Joe? I love it here, but I . . . I want to go home."

"So do I, my love." He looked at Levi then Simon. "How long can you be here? I need to finish up some things at The Temple. I don't want to just walk off the job. I'd like to go together if we could. I could use your support."

"You've got it." Simon gave a firm nod. Simon had grown up in the past year. "Right Levi?"

"Of course."

"Then we leave for Nazareth in three days time. That should be enough."

Mary glowed and I felt the warmth of her happy heart all the way to where I stood behind the gate. I settled into the straw and slept the slumber of those who work hard, love their people, and do what they can in service to all The Most High loves.

Oh, never forget the love of The Most High, friend. I sleep the sleep of those who know they are beautifully loved by a beautiful God.

We did not love
in vain.

Chapter Nine

Two Turtle Doves

You might be wondering why I'm still here, after fourteen hundred years. Well, simply put, I was rewarded by an angel for my faithfulness. "You shall not die until you bear the Lord's Messiah into Jerusalem."

I didn't know what any of that meant then. But I sure do now. And that time came when Jesus was still an infant.

Everyone's asleep, so come aside for a bit and let me tell you how it happened, for my time on this earth is drawing to a close and don't you feel one bit sad for me! Maybe I never roamed the open fields and hills like I longed to do, but I have been loved more than a little jenny like me ever thought possible. The Most High loves the animals too, everybody. We all deserve kindness. Please, please, please, jot that down.

Here we go.

In the land of Israel, women must wait forty days after giving birth to a baby boy before heading out into the world again. They call this being unclean. People use that word a lot in these parts. Some people go around unclean for their entire lives either because of physical problems, the work they do, or they just don't care. There are plenty of people who don't care in Israel. If you picture a nation where everyone is devout, you'd be wrong. And being a donkey, who am I to judge? All I know is, my people are good people, kind people, just people. Clean or unclean.

The forty days of Mary's confinement had ended and finally, good humans, the day for me to bear the Messiah had arrived! Bray and bray and bray! Altogether now, The Messiah is here!

The Messiah was coming to Jerusalem for the very first time in the arms of his parents, to The Temple that would take him in like it did young Samuel the prophet, to the people oppressed by Rome who could use a great light, the light of the Gentiles, too. That part isn't going to go over big, I can tell you that. People in these whereabouts don't like Gentiles for the most part and unfortunately, their dislike—repulsion is more like it—has made them ripe to believe it's them against everybody else.

I've seen it many times in my long life.

Jesus' parents readied him. We planned to take the busy road from Bethlehem to Jerusalem to present him to God and to offer Mary and Joe's sacrifice at the temple, two turtledoves.

Mary sat upon my back, Jesus cradled in her arms. Joe took my reins. "Ready, Issy?"

I squeaked. I had been ready for centuries. I've walked the Silk Road from east to west and back again more times than I remember. I've trod the grain mills, waged war upon the plain of Armageddon, traipsed the countryside with a young Nazarene woman and carried her to Hebron and Bethlehem.

I waited for this Messiah longer than any one being on this planet did, for are not humankind's days like grass? Do they not flourish like the flowers of the field only to have the wind of time pass over them, plucking away their petals, drying their youth, rendering them to dust?

Not so with Old Is. I bore The Messiah to Jerusalem, just like the angel said I would. The promise was made! The promise to me, just a little donkey, was finally being fulfilled.

I tell you this, you who read my tale of The Messiah, The Most High keeps every promise made. Adonai, the name the people of Israel will speak, will never turn away from that which comes to pass or will come to pass. Because the great love of God, the compassion of The Creator springs up anew each morning.

I wasn't the only one receiving the fulfillment of a promise that day.

Simeon was there too.

It was a good time for that sort of thing, to be certain.

Simeon believed in the coming of that day and it was counted to him as righteousness. That's what always happens to those who believe the promises of The Most High who watches over us and loves us all.

What is righteousness, you might ask? Having seen a lot of humans all these years, I have my own definition. It is knowing you are a good gift from The Most High and passing it through to others by recognizing the good gift they are and treating them as you would treat God if God stood before you in flesh.

Well, that was happening right then. God In Flesh was with us. God was on my back. And God had always had my back. I saw it then. Every bit of it.

God In Flesh was entering The Temple as a baby. And if Jesus did that, so must we wall. Come as little children, everybody! You don't have to know anything ahead of time, simply trust God each day!

The roads were crowded and the going slow, but I don't mind slow going. We all get there eventually, wherever "there" happens to be.

Through the gates and into the Holy City we walked. We passed Antonia, the Roman garrison attached to The Temple and held as an abomination by most Jews, and to the gateway of the outer courts. Yep, that Roman eagle was displayed above it letting all the worshippers know they were only there because the Emperor said it was all right. *So don't go thinking too highly of yourselves, or your god, for that matter.*

Oh, Rome. Someday you too will fall. Proud nations always do eventually, blinded by the lies they tell themselves. Usually God or god factors in highly.

But that day, none of that mattered. The massive stones, the colorful robes, even the noise stirred my donkey heart.

How beautiful are your courts, oh, Most High God.

My long-gone friend, King David, penned those words.

Near the entrance, Joe employed a street boy to watch over me. Thin and begrimed, the lad climbed up on my back, circled his arms around my neck and fell asleep. Better a donkey than a stone pavement! I peeked into the courtyard.

Men sat behind tables stacked with coins to trade local currencies into temple coinage. A simple beast like me failed to see the difference between the two, but what do I know? Animals stood together in makeshift pens and cages, ready to be bought. Only five were acceptable: bulls, sheep, goats, doves, and pigeons. Donkeys not acceptable. Not that I have any problem with that! God knows we have enough to deal with.

Mary and Joe purchased a pair of turtle doves, an acceptable sacrifice to deliver Mary out of the ritual uncleanliness which prohibited her from touching anything holy. On that day, she would be fully cleansed, resurrected back into society.

As a mother now, too!

For even the mother of The Messiah needed the redemption He was bringing to all of us.

What an honor to continue God's desire that life should go on.

Despite the rules, however, it behooves me to say (and only donkeys should be allowed to use that word!) she touched something holy over and over again as she cared for Jesus. But this was a land of laws, laws, and more laws. So to The Temple we must go!

Joe, like his family, was an expert in the law and so he was called *Just*. He kept the laws faithfully, so faithfully not even the most hardened person would have dreamed of asking him to do otherwise. That's what consistency will do for a human!

Thankfully, God doesn't ask these sorts of things from donkeys. And some of the requirements the humans keep? Between you and me, I have to wonder about them. Of course, humans are way more prone to get in trouble and justify it than we donkeys.

Beyond the outer court rested inner courts, inner-inner courts, and finally, the Holy of Holies. Only the High Priest gets to go in there to meet God. And only once a year. It's a good thing for me God isn't *only* in there, for The Most High has always been with me, a little beast of burden, small in stature but Olympian in love. God knows how much I have needed The Holy Presence each day during so long a life, and not an easy one at that.

Sometimes people received the meat back from their offerings, but this kind of sacrifice did not apply. It would go to the priests.

The family disappeared into the inner courts. I settled in, happy to have the company of the sleeping boy. Rest now, little child of Abraham, I thought. Perhaps you are not received by prophets and priests today, and maybe just a donkey will have to do, but you are loved just the same. And it's the everlasting love of The Most High that holds you in its arms. Rest.

I got a little drowsy too.

I heard the rest of the story later as Mary and Joe recounted the tale to Jacob and Ruth, Joe's parents. Standing at the stable gate, I listened in, my heart glowing with an understanding of my new, unknown friend and brother-in-waiting, Simeon of The Temple.

"He met us on the steps and reached out," Mary said, ladling the stew she had made for the household earlier that day. "I didn't know what he wanted, but he said, 'The babe. Is this the Promised One?'"

"You could have pushed me over with a breath at that point," Joe said. "'You mean The Messiah?' I asked him."

"And he did!" Mary set down the large bowl of the warm stew for everyone. "He told us God had promised he would see him before he died! And somehow he recognized Jesus as that one. Did an angel whisper in his ear?"

It turned out I wasn't the only one promised to see The Promised One before my life ended! Although, may I just add that one lifetime as opposed to fourteen hundred years is quite the difference. But then humans are more impatient than donkeys. But Simeon and I were promised the same thing, and those who receive the same promises from God are linked by a scarlet thread. Do you know what that thread is?

Hope and trust and experiences of God's faithfulness all entwined together and the stronger for it.

"He is The Messiah," Jacob, Joe's father, said. "The Prince of Peace has come and he is sleeping upstairs."

A sharp, happy shout resounded down the hole cut through the ceiling.

"Well, he *was*." Mary held a hand up to her mouth to stifle her laugh. "I'll get him."

Joe stood up. "No, Mary. You eat. I'll hold him until you're finished."

And so it was a good time for it. Just like every household where a welcomed child has entered needing the love and care of its parents.

The tale of Anna the Prophetess emerged after Mary had eaten half her bowl. "She's eighty-four years old and has lived at The Temple for years and years, ever since she was a young widow. Anyway, she clearly knows what it means that The Messiah has been born. She spoke and prophesied and preached about him!"

Ruth drew in a breath.

"She did, Mother," Joe said. "You should have heard her. 'The Light has come,' she said. It was as if Isaiah himself stood on the steps with us."

"From a woman!" his mother said.

Joe laughed. "And she wasn't even technically allowed to do so!"

Mary nodded. "Yes. The very first message in The House of God concerning God's gift, come into the world. Given by a woman."

I wanted to bray. We jennies clearly don't get enough credit, human or donkey, but we get the word out nonetheless and the word is this:

Jesus is born. The Word is here. The Son of God is with us. Immanuel! God in Flesh.

For all the people!

Glory of Israel. Light of the Gentiles.

That's the whole world. And trust me, you *really* want to jot that one down!

Take note, good humans. If you realize this all-loving God for yourself and others, everything will change. Because a world The Messiah deems worth coming to is a world worth living in and believe me, I've lived here long enough to know.

I once heard Shekinah, the glory of God, had never come again after Solomon's Temple was destroyed. Having been on the donkey crew during its construction, I knew that the second temple also held a stone for the Ark of the Covenant which was said to have held the Shekinah. But, of course, no Ark ever entered its portals.

In flesh yet still the Glory of Israel and that which carried it until the day it should be delivered arrived to a mighty Temple, but yet incomplete.

Until now.

The Ark and the Glory returned and I brought them. Me. Old Is. God works in the strangest of ways. Let me tell you. Is your pen still handy?

As for you, Bethlehem of
Ephrathah, even though you
remain least among the clans
of Judah, nevertheless, the
one who rules in Israel for me
will emerge from you. His
existence has been from
antiquity, even from eternity.

Micah 5:2
(JUB)

Chapter Ten

I slept, apparently, for Joe awakened me again the next morning and began readying me. I had been dreaming of sailing among the stars. Imagine! A donkey traveling the universe with The Most High.

I ate and drank, readying for a day of work, hopefully not hard work, but one never knows. And nobody asks me what *I* want.

Mary entered. "Do you think it will happen? Do you think we will go home?"

Joe reached out and held her cheek. "Oh, my love. I don't know. But God has led us so far. I don't see that changing."

She looked down. "I'm trusting. I just want it my way, I guess. It's hard not to."

"As long as we tend to God's leading, we can want what we want, but that doesn't mean we'll get it."

"And most of the time that's a good thing!" Mary laughed, then held up her hands. "All right, all right. I understand."

They embraced. Oh the feeling that pours out of people who love each other when they connect sure is a good one!

Joe turned to me. "Ready, girl?"

I squeaked out as soft a bray as possible.

"Issy!" Jesus sped through the gate and Mary scooped him up and onto her hip.

He pointed at me. "Ride tonight! Ride tonight?"

From the table, Simon let out his great laugh.

We would ride that night. But Jesus wouldn't be with us.

That evening (the day was much like others before it so why bore you?) after we had stayed late to pick up some extra pay, we returned with news of the Parthians.

Joe took care of me first, bless him, then hurried into the house. "Mary! Father, Mother! Hello, Levi, Simon." He wiped a forearm across his sweaty brow. "I heard more in Jerusalem today!"

"Have a seat, son." Jacob patted the bench next to him.

"What is it?" asked Ruth who had just come back from the communal oven with some hot bread.

"How was your day, Joe?" Mary called down from upstairs.

"It was fine, but there's news about the Parthians and I think it might concern us."

Mary descended the stairs snuggled against the wall, Jesus in her arms. "He's clean and fed." She deposited him into Ruth's outstretched arms. "What did you hear? Do we need fear?"

"I don't know. I don't even know if the story is true, but apparently, they want to see the new king of the Jews. They said they saw a star in the east and had come to *worship* him."

"Who did they say that to?" Mary asked.

"They went straight to the palace."

"To *Herod?* I'll bet he *loved* hearing that." Jacob picked up a piece of the hot bread, his tekton fingers so calloused from all his years of working with stone the heat meant nothing.

"Apparently he's got all the scholars combing old scrolls for prophecies concerning where 'this king' should be born."

Mary's eyes rounded. "Will it be here?"

Ruth, who had studied the law in her home growing up as long as she could, who had continued with the prophets through her grandfather, who had, with Jacob, passed the knowledge down to her son, said, "'But you Bethlehem Ephratah though you be little among the thousands of Judah, out of you shall come forth he who will be ruler of Israel.'"

"Micah," said Joe.

"Yes, dear. Micah."

"Anyway, I don't know what this means. The news was that Herod told the magi when they found this king to let him know so he could come and worship him too."

"What a bunch of rot," said Simon, as he sat down to eat. "Herod? As if that would happen. He was probably disappointed it wasn't him to begin with."

Levi grimaced, sitting down too. "He probably thinks it *is* him. Pity those scholars. I hope they don't end up dead for revealing the truth of the matter."

Everyone stilled as Ruth handed Jesus to his grandfather. "He needs to be changed again."

Jacob sighed. "Oh." His eyes darted around seeking rescue. Nobody. "All right."

"I'll do it, Abi." Joe took Jesus who looked as if he was one minute from being done with the pass around. Jesus nestled into him. Joe sighed as if all the cares of the day were suddenly washed away.

Ruth and Mary began setting out the meal.

I was glad for my stable bed. While we were gone the old straw had been swept away and new straw strewn about.

"Perhaps we really should go home," Mary said. Mary had known despair in all of this and it had been turned to joy. But now . . . everything shifted once more to the realm of the unknown. She dropped her head, set down a stack of bowls, then rubbed her eyes and whispered a prayer of David. "'My heart and flesh may fail me, but God is my strength and my portion.'"

Jesus decided to sleep, despite Joe's wiping. His young body was supple, yielding like a willow branch. He was unaware of the possible storm that had settled upon them with the coming of these wise men from the east. It was only a matter of time before they arrived, before they saw their young Messiah, and before they returned to Jerusalem to tell Herod of his whereabouts.

"How do you think they will find him here in Bethlehem?" asked Simon. "It's not as if you all have been parading him through the streets as the coming king."

"His birth caused a bit of a fuss. People will remember," said Mary.

"It will be all right," Ruth declared. "He will grow up, controlled by no man, free to do the perfect will of Adonai. He has to. God knows that."

"Yes, yes." Joe stood up with Jesus in his arms. "Here, Mary, take Jesus. I'm going out."

"Where?"

"To find them myself. If they've come to worship our son, if they did the honorable thing and asked Herod, they're good men. They don't mean harm, they aren't spies. The Most High sent them." He made for the stable gate and I stepped aside. "And that means they've come for a good reason. I'm taking Issy."

Mary laid her hand on his arm. "Why? Isn't she tired after a long day?"

Oh, Mary, you love me.

Joe rubbed and patted my cheeks and scratched my ears. "What do you say, Issy?"

I squeaked and nodded my head, an over-nod yes, but I was that excited. Magi! I knew magi.

"I still don't know why she can't stay and rest. She works so hard," said Mary.

"Issy's good protection. I probably won't need it, but if I do, there's nobody I would rather have by my side then this girl."

You need me and I am at the ready, Joe!

Because don't forget everybody. Donkeys fight with their front legs *and* their back legs. I wouldn't fail him. Not for a minute. Not for a single breath.

Well, yes. I suppose I am a little vain.

Chapter Eleven

Finding Magi

"Let's head to the Jerusalem Road, Issy."

Joe took my reins and we walked through the narrow streets of Bethlehem. The night chill didn't bother me, but it seemed to be making Joe shiver. He took a lot of deep breaths and I couldn't blame him. For the simple Jew, everything having to do with Herod felt like a risk. Such a difficult time, such an oppressive place for The Messiah to be born.

Then again . . . what better time can there be for a deliverer? Even his name means such. "God saves."

Now if you jot down nothing else but that, you'd be all the better for it.

"I'm not going all the way to Jerusalem," he said out loud as though everybody chatted with their preferred beast, highly preferred in this case. "And the truth is, if anybody has already seen the magi around here, we'll end up hearing about it. I know, let's go to the well."

King David cried out one day, "If only I could drink from the well of Bethlehem, the place of my birth." I know because I heard him say it. I've heard some things in my time even from the "man after God's own heart." He was a stinker, and yet God loved him like a cherished son. And he, in turn, loved his own cherished son, who was an even bigger stinker than he was.

That's what love does for a person.

The difference between David and a lot of people was that he admitted when he wronged someone, when he had failed to keep the law, to love the Lord God with all his heart, soul, mind, and strength. That's all God wants from humans. The Most High knows the likes of you bald-bodied creatures have a hard time being just and upright all the time. But God would rather humans just be honest about it. God knows exactly what the person on the other end feels like, you see. Humans aren't fooling The Almighty. They just think if they move on, God might not notice. Or not care. But God hears the suffering cry of the oppressed, the used, and the reviled. God hears the songs of broken hearts, the one whose will went unconsidered, even the one who made mistakes and lived to bear the consequences. David knew that.

Joe sucked in his breath.

And there they were!

Don't be thinking this was luck. Most travelers ended up at the well. "We're in luck!" Joe said anyway.

I snorted and raised up my head.

He chuckled. "You're right. Luck had nothing to do with it."

To say the traveling train of what we came to call The Three Kings in our household was lavish would be akin to calling the Coliseum in Rome *big*. Well, yes. Of course.

Joe saw the priests when I did. "There." He pointed subtly. "Look at those men, Issy. My goodness."

These priests weren't hurting for anything The Most High provides. Even though daylight was fading, silks shone like a fluttering prism there at the north end of town. The breezes from the wilderness just beyond the well scoured the hard earth and moved anything of little substance in its cool breath.

"I wonder if Bethlehem has ever seen the like," Joe whispered.

Camels drank as servants drew more water. The peculiar, cone-shaped hats of the Parthians shone in torchlight or were silhouetted against the night sky. Jingling jewelry, elaborate swords, and bells on harnesses sung a song of wealth and ownership of centuries.

Joe worked on villas of wealthy people in Sepphoris, people who had followed the Greek or Roman mode of the day in sumptuous simplicity. He was used to walking among the wealthy.

But not so the magi!

They came from the land of the rising sun, simplicity not required, lavishness obtained. "I know! Let's decorate that!" should be the region's motto. I brayed at the sight of the life I once had for two hundred years, decorated and cared for, a trader of beautiful things along the Silk Road.

The magi turned at the sound of my excited bray. I just couldn't help myself. It had been so long.

Joe raised a hand. He hurried over and said five words.

"I know where he is."

They stilled.

They maintained their composure.

But one priest, a middle-aged man with shiny red boots and a cape of white fur, laughed and clasped the shoulder of another man, old and looking like he just began rising from a chair, only he hadn't. "I told you El Elyon would show us the way, didn't I, Balthazzar?"

"You did, Casper. But I was hoping God would preserve my aching back a little for all this effort."

"Excuse—" Joe began.

"El Elyon helps those who help themselves," said a woman who sat upon the smallest camel I had ever seen saddled up. She was almost as beautiful as my Mary, her eyes tilted toward the moon, her lips as red as Casper's boots.

The third priest, younger than the others, pulled a small leather sack from his camel, a giant beast with two humps. "Here, take some of this. I got it from an old woman in—"

"Don't try to pawn off your strange herbs on me, young man!" said Balthazzar. "I wasn't born—"

"Yesterday. Yes, I know. But this will take the edge off. They're just herbs."

"Excu—" Joe.

"No. Thank you, Melchior, but no."

There are always people who refuse such things and there always will be, I suppose. If I have seen it once, I have seen the refusal to feel better a thousand, no, make that ten thousand, times.

Melchior returned the sack. "Suit yourself. I've got it if you need it. Casper? What do you say? Should we follow this rough-handed fellow and his jenny?"

He knew! Bless you, Melchior!

I have been called a jackass too many times.

"Finally," Joe whispered, thinking only I could hear.

The woman smiled and patted her camel, her bracelets singing to her black hair that danced along with her turquoise veil. "Come on, little camel. You've had your fill. Let's follow this nice young man and see if what he says is true."

"Don't get too comfortable up there, Meili," Caspar said. He turned to Joe, "Melchior's wife comes with us sometimes."

"That sounds very nice," said Joe. "Would you like to follow me?"

Casper directed a young male servant to take the camel's reigns. "This is my camel. He's like a brother to me."

And I saw it! I saw the beaming, happy pride in the camel's eyes and I knew he knew far more than he could, or perhaps would, say. Zebby was like Old Is, wise beyond a beastly ken. Perhaps we could swap tales.

As they passed us, Zebby whispered (in Camelus, of course), "Hello, Starlight. I'm not surprised to see you."

"Do I know you?"

"I'm Zebby, the Noble Camel. Your legend has been told by the animals far and wide ever since you disappeared from the routes years ago. And here you are. So it's true. You were meant to bear the king who should be worshipped. The king who is the Son of The Highest God of all. Have you?"

I dropped my head. "I have."

"And?"

"Come see for yourself. I imagine if God sent the favored Son for humans, we get to join in the song."

"You believe that?"

"I know it. Just you wait, Zebby. You'll feel it too."

The woman laughed. "Why I'd think these two creatures were talking to each other."

Joe shrugged. "Ma'am, please excuse me if I am being impertinent, but stick around and this will be the least of the amazing things you will see."

"True?"

"I promise." Joe turned to the magi. "Are you ready?"

"We are," said Melchior.

"Then let's go."

Joe stopped. "Oh, and I think we'd all appreciate it if you didn't bring all the others. It's a small house."

Of course, there were onlookers.

He did
not run in
vain.

Chapter Twelve

The home of Jacob and Ruth became a palace receiving room that night. Zebby, who had invited himself into the stable from the stableyard (I didn't mind) stood next to me at the inner gate.

Mary pointed at us. "Those two make a perfect picture."

Zebby's eyes grew and he spoke again. Good thing I know Camelus! "My goodness. Who is that?"

"The mother of The Promised One."

Zebby gasped. "She's so very beautiful. And there's something about her, it's peaceful yet strong, supple yet determined."

I gaped at him. "Well, aren't you a fancy talker?"

He snickered. "The fanciest."

Oh, I liked this camel!

The light from the fire and the oil lamps ricocheted off of the finery, the gleaming skin of the magi and the beautiful women. "Who is she?" I asked Zebby as introductions began.

"She's a stargazer, too. From the far east. She saw a portent star a year ago and found Melchior. He's renowned for that sort of thing. He fell for her and who can blame him? Why she agreed to marry him, I cannot begin to comprehend."

I brayed a laugh.

"He's a fine stargazer in his own right, although"—Zebby leaned his head closer to mine—"he's young. He could learn quite a bit from my master and that old man."

"Balthazzar?"

"Yes. I find him tiresome. Not because he's old and bent, but because, like his back, he is set in his ways."

"Are you?" I asked.

Zebby shook his head. "No. I can't be. Caspar is the most adventurous of the three of them. We go everywhere together."

"Do you see Mary over there? It was the same way with her. Until she had the baby."

"That's always the way, isn't it?"

"Yes, but I don't mind. I like all of them. And we take fine walks where I am allowed to walk without reins or my harness."

"So you, the grand trader, found a home among stonemasons?"

"More than that, Zebby. They're builders of the grand kingdom of The Most High. At least that's the way I see it. And that little baby there is the cornerstone of it all."

Zebby peered at Jesus who was running around tugging on the robes of magi, pointing to me and shouting, "Issy! Come see Issy!" just like any other vocal toddler wanting to show off what he loves.

"How can you be sure?"

"Angels. Angels have been around this whole thing for a long time now."

Zebby lowered himself to the ground. "I believe you, Starlight."

I stayed standing, happy to have a newfound friend. Maybe he'd pick up that my name was now Issy. Then again, maybe not.

The humans chattered softly as Mary told the magi the entire story, from Gabriel's visit to her onward. Meilie and Balthazzar sat at the table with Mary, and the rest of the men settled down on the ground near the fire. Ruth gathered cups and set out wine.

"My goodness," she whispered to Joe. "Has Bethlehem ever seen the like?"

"Not that I know of, Mother. Has Israel?"

"Only conquering kings seem to come our way like this," she said.

"Perhaps those days are over." Joe began pouring wine.

"Or perhaps not," Zebby said to me. "This is a different king. He needs not swords and spears. His very word will heal the nations."

"Where did you hear that?" I know my mouth gaped, but wasn't The Messiah called to champion Israel?

"I heard my master say it after reading deeply our prophecies. He will be that powerful, Issy. Make no mistake."

I wanted to believe him, but . . .

Wait!

"The Prince of Peace," I said.

Our attention was captured by the scene as Mary finished up the story. "So here we are."

Jesus slid off her lap. "Issy!" He pointed to me.

"Oh, all right," said Ruth, opening the gate. "You can play with Issy."

I sat down and he climbed up onto my back. "Ride, Issy!"

"So you're actually from Nazareth?" asked Caspar.

Mary smoothed her robe. "Yes. We were planning to head back soon. What do you think about Herod?"

"I don't trust him at all," said Melchior.

"Nor I," agreed Balthazzar.

Caspar shrugged. "Not surprisingly. Herod's reputation isn't exactly obscure in our part of the world. But nevertheless, the scholars he consulted seemed to see it all in a day's work."

Of course, townspeople began to gather outside the house. One fellow actually peered in the window of the stable. Zebby turned and spat in his direction. He quickly pulled away and I heard him say, "That camel just spit on me!" in a sort of shock.

I squeaked a laugh. "Good one, Zeb."

"Thank you kindly, Starlight."

Caspar suddenly arose from the table and came to the gate. "Noble Friend," he said. "Rise."

Zebby did his master's bidding right away.

Caspar reached up to Zebby's packs and pulled out a chest of gleaming olive wood carved with leaves and monkeys. Hinges decorated with lines swirling into clouds held it together.

Melchior stepped outside and returned with an elegant stone jar, Greek, because as Zebby later whispered, "Melchior likes to show off that he travels far and wide. He also thinks he has better taste than the others because he likes simple, fine things."

And finally, old Balthazzar unfolded himself as much as possible and walked toward Mary. "We have gifts, you see."

"Jesus!" she called. "Come see what these nice men have brought!"

I wanted to laugh as hard as I ever have. "These nice men." Oh that was rich! Then again, Jesus was a King of kings, was he not? And this humble home? A palace.

Jesus hugged my neck, ran back into the house and allowed his mother to place him on her lap.

Balthazzar, lowering himself as if made of glass, bent his knees, bowed his head, and in hands as gnarled as a bristlecone pine he held aloft a ceramic urn, shaped by expert hands, elegant with a neck like a queen's.

Melchior knelt down with ease and presented the jar.

"Gold for a king," said Caspar, doing the same.

"Frankincense for a priest." Balthazzar bowed his head.

"Myrrh for the man," Melchior said the words with authority.

The traditional gifts to give to royalty. Given to Apollo himself it was said.

"They really believe he's a king," I said to Zebby.

"He is." The camel stood up, placed a foot forward and lowered his head over his knee. "They're good people, bound to what is true not what they think should be true or wish would be true. They wouldn't be doing this if they weren't sure. Why would they?"

This baby, yes. I knew. Mary knew. Joe knew. Everyone in the house knew. But now I knew something else. There were others, and more would follow and more and more because this was God's Son here, in flesh, like us.

Why? I asked The Most High in my heart. Why are You doing this?

Because it's a good time for it.

That's right! This was foretold! The day would come when the dark was so dark it could not understand the Light! But the Light had come. The Light has come! And darkness from here on out is abolished. For this Light demands it and commands it to utterly disband it. Oh, humans might take a while to realize it, of course. Especially if they refuse to open their eyes. But that doesn't mean it is not so.

Meilie knelt down and took Jesus' little hands in hers. "I have nothing fine to give him, but I give him love."

Jesus leaned forward and grabbed her face like he did his mother's. "Like her! Love her." And pulled her toward him for a kiss on her cheek.

When Meilie straightened back up tears shown like sweet fires in her beautiful black eyes.

We did not give in vain.

Chapter Thirteen

Time to Go

The next morning, before the moon had begun to lose its shine, the esteemed guests who had decided to take Jacob's offer to sleep in the guest room above the stable awakened with such a startled cry, all the animals were pulled from their slumber.

Voices descended down the ladder, unascertainable as to content, but filled with meaning.

"Goodness," said Zebby.

"I feel it too," I said.

Five minutes later Melchior practically jumped down from the opening, his heels barely touching a rung until he stood, still somewhat sprung, in the middle of the room. "I'll get Balthazzar."

The old priest slept in the main room before the fire. No ladders for him anymore. As Melchior jostled him, he started shouting in his sleep.

"Shh!" said Melchior. "Old man, shh!"

Balthazzar opened his eyes. "Lad. Why are you waking me up from my grand dream? I walk perfectly in my dreams, you know."

"Caspar had a dream."

"Oh, well, why are you waking *me* up?"

Zebby whispered, "Caspar dreams dreams."

"Ahh," I said, no stranger to dreamers.

"He was warned to go home a different route. He was told not to tell Herod where Jesus is residing."

Balthazzar raised himself onto an elbow as Meilie made her way down the ladder with a careful ease. "Do you think we should leave now? Are we in danger?"

"I don't know."

Caspar walked by us and over to the other priests. "I think we'll be fine. I was told not to engage Herod further. There could be a lot of reasons for that. And to be clear, I would rather not become too closely acquainted with him. Our lands don't need the likes of him and I'd like to keep it that way."

Balthazzar laid back down. "Five more minutes?"

"We'll get everything ready to go. Sleep on."

"But what about my breakfast?"

Zebby whispered. "He's not the brightest star of the three, especially lately, and especially in the morning."

Joe awakened where he, Mary, and Jesus had been sleeping near Heffy. Caspar filled him in on what was going on. Mary heard. Jesus slept.

Ruth entered the room. "I just heard. We have some bread and wine. There are olives and some cheese, too. I'll lay it out for you."

"I'll help," offered Meilie.

"That would be lovely, dear." Ruth handed her a knife.

Zebby stood. "I might as well prepare myself." He walked toward the watering trough where other camels were gathering.

Simon, asleep in the stable with us, began to rise. "I'll get more water. Issy? Want to go to the well?"

Good heavens! A wise man dreams a dream and we all have to hop to! Ah, well. I walked toward him. "See you in a little while, Zebby."

But Zebby was already getting into his proud camel mode. A servant came to put on his silks and harness and arrange his packs. He didn't even hear my words.

I didn't mind, though. I was heading out with Simon! I had known this lively human for years now, one of Mary's favorite people and one of mine too, even if he did desert her on the road to Nazareth before he believed her story about Gabriel. I had a hard time forgiving that one, I did. But then, I'm a donkey. We're not exactly known for being wishy-washy creatures, are we?

We went to the well three times before the train of beasts were watered, fed, and ready to head not to the north and eventually meet up with the Silk Road, but south.

"It will be a long trip around the Dead Sea," said Joe as Caspar told him their plan.

"It will. But I've learned to listen to dreams."

Joe laughed out loud. "You're not the only one around here!"

The group had eaten, but Ruth tucked bread in some of Mary's clean, woven cloth. "For the road," she said. All expressed gratitude.

I watched it all from the stable door as they prepared to go, helping Balthazzar onto a donkey, a white jack with an eye for the jennies if last night was any indication. Meilie was about to be boosted up onto Zebby when Caspar stopped her. "Just a moment, if you please."

He walked around to Zebby and spoke words I couldn't hear to the camel. Zebby didn't move. When Caspar was finished, he patted Zebby's head, placed his cheek against the camel's and closed his eyes. And then, much to the surprise of all, he led Zebby back into the stable of Jacob and Ruth.

"Zebby!" I said. "What?"

Zebby closed his eyes. "He says the new king might have need of me."

"Why?"

"I don't know." Zebby lowered himself into the straw, and if he had been a human, he would have cried. I could feel it. "I don't know," he said again.

I walked toward the courtyard. "You don't want to see them go?"

"No." He turned his face toward the wall.

The entourage was gone just as the sun crested the hills. Ruth and Mary cleaned up. Jesus still slept.

"Well, you have a camel too, among other things," Ruth said with a laugh.

"They truly treated Jesus like a king!" Mary wiped down the table as Ruth gathered the blankets upon which Balthazzar laid.

Ruth folded each piece of fabric and stacked them onto the bench. "Let's hope you won't need that little beast for his speed like they think you might."

"The old priest said he's faster than any horse he's ever seen. Isn't that amazing?"

I turned to Zebby. "See? You're here because you're fast. In case we ever need to get away quickly."

Zebby sighed and laid his chin upon the straw.

I do nothing in vain.

Chapter Fourteen

A Madman Goes About His Business

The next morning the big discussion centered on whether or not we should head to Jerusalem to work. Joe stood firm. "We cannot hide here. And until Adonai says otherwise, we continue life as usual. Besides, there might be more to be found out. I'm just any other Jew there, Mary"—she looked unconvinced—"believe me."

By the time we returned home, Zebby had been relieved of his silks and finery. Neighbors stopped by to inquire about the visitors the night before and the family, being who they were, told the truth. The visitors had learned about the baby in their prophecies and came to see if it was true. Nobody mentioned worship. Everyone knew better.

The woman next door, Rhoda, had been watching everything since the night of Jesus' birth. One of the shepherds, Nathan, was her son. She came over that evening to bear witness and learn more, and she had a tale of her own. She collected her robes and the family around her and sat near the fire.

"I was in Jerusalem today. The good news is, the people are relieved the magi are gone. The bad news is, Herod isn't. In fact, he's raging at the palace. Everybody there is doing all they can to calm him."

Lest he turn his wrath on them!

Human beings think The Most High is like this. They do all sorts of things to placate the One who made them and loves them. It's highly unnatural to think of God so harshly, but for some reason the animals have yet to figure out, it feels right to them. Don't ask me!

Perhaps they just want God to punish their enemies, not redeem them.

Now let me tell you a little about Herod so you might understand. He conquered Israel for Rome about thirty years ago. He kills people like others kill flies. His own wife and two children were not immune to his crazed wrath, his unbalanced view of the world. He killed them all. Power does that to some men, but a lot of people said his body was filled with sickness, too. The king was always in pain, always bearing up under some form of bitter and even putrid malady. He was not well in mind, body, and certainly not in his human heart. Oh, no! None of it worked well. He was no more fit to govern than any man of vengeance is, for vengeance belongs to The Most High. Herod did oversee building projects well, though. Perhaps he should have been an architekton and left it at that.

It's important to know your calling and Herod was living proof. I'm rather positive this kind of thing will repeat itself well into the future. But this baby gives me hope, nevertheless.

"It isn't over, I can tell you that." Levi stood at the door of the house shaking the dust of the day from his outer robe. "Anybody else?" Simon, of course, took off his robe and handed it over.

Rhoda nodded. "It isn't. Apparently, Herod is sending spies here tomorrow."

Yep, palace servants love to spread news such as this.

"Why spies?" asked Ruth. "Can't he just ask people if they saw the magi?"

"That would make too much sense," said Jacob. "He should have had someone just follow the magi to see where they ended up."

Mary, who was watching over Jesus as he played with a set of flat, creek stones, said, "*That* would make too much sense."

See? The man was living in crazy village.

"It would also be disrespectful to the magi. Perhaps he was smart enough to know they would realize they were being followed," said Joe, always willing to give people the benefit of the doubt. "And the last thing we need is to have the Parthians try to rule us again. Because the magi could be spying to see whether or not they could pull off taking Israel again. Finding a new king from Israel to rule Israel but with the best interest of the Parthians in mind. Sort of a coup from within."

"Herod's mind would definitely go to that spot," agreed Mary.

"Not to mention that if war breaks out under his watch in this little country? Rome would have a fit. And he'd be out."

"That makes sense. And to offer his own men to accompany them? Why not that?" asked Simon.

"It could be seen as insulting, a sign of suspicion, too," said Levi, beginning to shake out Simon's robe. "Either way, he didn't. If he had, would God have given Caspar a dream?"

At the mention of Caspar's name, Zebby sighed.

The speculative conversation continued, but I had some hospitality to keep here in my stable. I folded myself next to Zebby. "How are you doing, Zebby?"

"How would you be doing?"

"Terrible. I love my family and I assume you loved your master."

"Loved? Love. I love my master. Born right in his stables I was. I opened the womb of my mother."

Let me inform you of something. In the times wherein I was born and into the present day of where I came to be, there was something special about a male offspring being the one that opens the womb of a female. It came to be a sacred thing, but I always suspected it was more of a cause for relief, a check off the list. The family would go on. The house would stand. The fields would ripen with harvest. The work would go on into the next generation. That's the way it was in a culture where brute strength always won the day, no matter the type of field upon which it was displayed—battle or barley.

"He loved me from the start," Zebby said. "From the very first day."

"How could he not?"

Zebby was a very beautiful creature, his coat glossy from years of daily brushing, his eyes, rimmed with thick lashes, clear from searching horizons, his nails filed perfectly.

"As you say," I said.

Zebby turned to look at me, sadness in his eyes. "I say that not because I am special, although I am small, yes. I say that because he is loving."

"Ah. Yes. Being loved makes all the difference, doesn't it?"

"And now, I'm just here, in this place. Unknown, unloved, unable to be of help. More water must be drawn, more food worked for to feed a hungry beast like me. What could my master have been thinking?"

"The Most High likely said so."

Zebby smiled at me. And by smile I mean sparkles raced across the slick surface of his great brown eyes. "He said as much."

"So then, all you must do is wait and see why The Most High has you here. Is that so bad?"

I don't know why I even asked that question. As if waiting in the cloud of unknowing is easy for anybody. I knew that first hand. Many centuries of waiting and not one year of it was easy in that regard.

"Zebby? I'm sorry. I should have remembered how hard it is. How even one day of it can be excruciating."

"You're the one who should feel *least* sorry for me, Starlight, after all those years?"

"Listen, new friend. If all those years taught me little in the way of compassion, they surely were wasted. And I hate to think that I've come through all of it only to scorn you."

"Thank you."

"I'm here. And I will help you. You don't have to go through this alone."

"I value that."

"Oh, and you are loved already. This family? They don't need an excuse to love. They love you because . . . you are. And you are here."

It was a good time for us to expand a little more. And why not have a camel in the family? Whyever not?

The next day, after we returned from work, Zebby stood at my gateway. He moved right over to make room for me.

"Oh look!" said Mary. "Isn't that the sweetest thing you've ever seen? Issy has a friend!"

I squeaked and Zebby, who had been given back his bells, shook them.

Jesus clapped. He ran toward the gate crying, "Zebby, Zebby, Zebby!"

Joe tapped the table. "Zebby! Why that's a fine name, Son. That's exactly what we'll call him."

Zebby and I looked at each other and we knew all we had been through, all we had been called and were called to do, was true.

"Somehow, he knows you by name, Zebby."

"I don't know why I am so surprised. Do you think he really knows it, or was it whispered to him deep in the recesses of his heart?"

"Does it matter?"

Zebby thought for several seconds. "No, I suppose it doesn't."

Zzzzzzz ...

Chapter Fifteen

Resting in Praise

Since moving to Bethlehem, the family joined hearts around the table in the evenings. And I joined in from the stable gate. Stable or table, did it matter? Not to The Most High! God was present and we all could feel it.

Everyone gathered had studied Torah as a child, memorizing the five books it housed. All Jewish children did, boys and girls. Both Mary and Ruth had gone on to privately study the prophets in the presence of their own fathers who believed that they should know the way The Most High communicates sometimes to God's children. In other words, they had their own thoughts on what Ezekiel and Isaiah meant and their thoughts were welcomed!

Something else entered in after the birth of Jesus when the family decided to stay in Bethlehem for a while. Song came forth from all of our hearts.

Mary had always loved to sing to herself and sing to God. But her song, as if birthed in the womb of that which gives humanity its form, its beauty, its purpose, extended to and through us all. Our household became filled with song each evening. Songs of David were sung each night. Some nights they wafted in softness around the table, and sometimes they filled the room to the rafters with abundant joy, almost raucous.

And Ruth and Jacob, mostly, would dance before the Lord.

In many ways, I wondered what would be revealed each day that showed Jesus was sent by The Most High.

Of course I realized, being as old as I am, that humans would forever seek to bring upon God their ways, their bents, as they all tend to do with anything even hinting at the Divine.

God is oftentimes more human than divine. But God is not fooled. The Most High lives and speaks not in our foolish ways of hiding or trying to pull the wool over the divine gaze that we are perfect, only joined to God in our goodness, left to bear our sins and sorrows alone. The Most High lives in the truth that is always ready to deliver us to the utmost.

These two families, both from the House of David, knew just like their royal forbear, that God was found most essentially in song. God's Spirit listened closely, drawing near to the room each night, like a mother.

Mary sang the words of David, "'How good it is to dwell in the courts of the Lord.'"

How good it was to sing.

Two nights after the departing of the priests, Zebby leaned into me and whispered. "Do they do this every night?"

"Almost."

"What is happening?"

"They're joining their hearts to God's."

"Ah."

"Do you wish to know how this is so, Zebby?"

"Perhaps. Will it help me?"

"Oh, yes. I assure you. The Almighty sings over all of creation, everything fashioned by the divine hand."

"The song of the spheres?" Zebby said. "Why even I know the stars themselves sing of the glory of God. That is what Caspar taught."

"How can it be otherwise?" I asked. "The glory of God is declared every night in the light of the stars that wink their way upon the web of space toward to earth. This family simply answers back. Tell us of the glory of God, they ask with their notes. Sing to us of the place where heaven touches us, here in our hearts, where we know You are. And let us offer You songs in return, may they fall pleasing upon Your ears, Adonai, and somehow, upon the creation itself."

"They bless and not curse?"

"They bless and not curse."

"Jesus joins in, of course. And in his play throughout the day, or so Mary says, he sings. He sings of everything he does as he does it."

"He does," Zebby agreed. "I've heard him."

Jesus. Bringing joy to the household in a land where freedom was held under the thumb of despots, and hope of deliverance had become merely the wishful thinking of a lot of people too frightened not to believe the promises of God. Not to believe in a God who they thought deep in their heart of hearts was worse than the emperor.

"God is love, though," I said.

"That was random, Issy."

I squeaked into a quiet bray. "Not according to my thoughts. Sorry about that."

"I'm sure you have many. Feel free to share them."

I focused on the family gathering and let their tune fall upon my ears.

"Oh, Lord, our Lord, how majestic is your name in all the earth."

Adonai, oh Adonai, you have brought the singer of your song, the north star in your sky, the breeze that cools our weary brow, the bearer of water that slakes our thirst forever. You have delivered our deliverer unto us.

"Amen," said Zebby.

I didn't realize I said the words aloud.

They were, indeed, the cry of my heart.

Jesus slipped down from his mother's lap, entered the stable through the gate and held out his small hand toward me. He walked toward my bed, squatted down as toddlers do, and patted the hay. "Issy! Sleep."

I left my station, and did his bidding. He curled up beside me, right in the crook of my neck and placed his little hand on my rounded cheek. Me, Old Is, bristled and worn, hardly the beautiful beast I had never been, actually. But that didn't seem to matter to Jesus.

He sighed and fell asleep.

Joe looked over the gate. "Like mother like son."

You better believe it, Joe. And I would guard him with my life just like I did my Mary. My fears were allayed. Clearly The Most High wasn't finished with me yet. The Lord *is* good. God's mercy endures forever.

We did not escape in vain!

Chapter Sixteen

The Flight!

"Issy!"

I rolled and rolled in the green green grass, beside the waters of life, the breezes of God releasing each strand of fur from the next, cooling my skin.

"Issy!"

The voice of The Most High sung in my ears, swirling around their shells and down into my brain. "You are loved. You are loved. You are loved. Issy, the donkey. Issy, Issy . . . "

"Issy!"

I came to in the night stable, Jesus now removed from my side. Zebby sat behind me. He perked up.

Joe whispered again. "Issy!"

I opened my eyes.

"We have to go. We have to get out of here and quickly!"

I climbed to my feet.

"Zebby, you too."

Joe must have realized Zebby was capable of understanding him as well.

Zebby unfolded his long, slender legs and stood.

Levi, a bit groggy, came in. "I heard Mary arise. It's the middle of the night, brother."

"I had a dream."

"First, what can I do? Second, tell me why I have done it, I ask."

Joe began harnessing me. "Saddle Zebby, if you don't mind. We have to leave. Hastily so. I was told we must go to Egypt, that Herod seeks the child's life."

Ruth and Jacob arose, Mary appeared with Jesus in her arms. Simon managed to crawl from his deep slumber and the place became a milling hive of silent bees, working, working, readying, readying.

Ruth and Jacob gathered everything the family would need to survive along the way. "We're all going, Son," said his father.

"That's right." Ruth began filling my baskets. "They will come here, and Herod will stop at nothing to get information out of us. I have no need of dying by the hand of that man this day or any other."

Jacob nodded. "We're in this together now. I don't know what Egypt holds, but I know whatever it holds for my son and his family, it holds for us. Simon? Levi? What about you?"

"Of course!" said Simon, smiling. "This might be our biggest adventure yet."

Levi nodded. "Yes. Many hands set to the field reap a bigger harvest. We'll need to survive once we get there. We'll need to preserve and grow this little one into the fullness to which he has been called."

"That's beautiful, brother." Mary laid a hand on his arm. "Thank you."

Joe stood tall and held up a hand. "It can't be like this. I am grateful for your willingness, everyone, but I can't allow you to put yourself in harm's way. Not to mention we need to move quickly. My home in Nazareth is still yours. Go there. There's work in Sepphoris, Father, as you know. Levi, perhaps you can get the two families together somehow."

Simon barked out a laugh. "Good luck with that!"

"Son, are you sure?" asked Ruth.

"It has to be this way." He turned to me. "Issy? We'll load you up as light as we possibly can. I know donkeys don't get much credit for speed—"

What? Now right there is a myth, everybody! We may not be able to outrun the fastest of horses, but when we want to run, we can. Make no mistake!

I brayed and tossed my head.

"Oh, Issy's fast!" said Mary. "Why one time, she got so spooked at a snake—"

I bowed my head. That story again?

I was soon loaded with the bare essentials: Joe's finer tools, Ruth's bread, water and wineskins, blankets, a cooking pot. Zebby was saddled and harnessed when a man—Nathan the young shepherd—burst through the door, terror stretching his face. "Herod's men are on the move! Old Ezekiel heard it from a priest come to view the flock yesterday. He told me as soon as I brought my flock to water. They will be coming at first light to try and root out The Messiah."

Joe took Mary's hand. "We can't get out of here quickly enough."

"They're going to come here," Simon said.

"Yes," Levi agreed. "But they won't find him."

Simon's mouth became a grim line. "Then Herod will take out his wrath on something else. Men like him, when they are unable to seek revenge on one, seek revenge on all."

"What do you mean, Simon?" asked Ruth.

"Just that I wish all the babies could be spirited away like Jesus right now."

Silence filled the room. Would even Herod do such a thing?

"Nathan, can you tell Ruth's family to come get the animals from the stable?" Jacob asked. "No life must remain inside these walls."

"Yes, consider it accomplished."

Once all was readied for the flight, Mary stood before me, Jesus strapped to her back. He was sleeping against her warmth. She took my face in her hands. "Issy, we're hastening away. And we need you, girl. We need you to run today."

I squeaked.

Joe's face came into view. "Issy, you have always been faithful. I know you can do this. And I am grateful, girl."

Oh, Joe, I love you.

He turned to Mary. "Are you ready, my dove?"

"We always do what we must and God always prepares the way," she reminded us all.

Jacob stepped forward. "We will head to Nazareth right away."

"We'll go through the wilderness," suggested Levi.

"Good thinking." Jacob moved to embrace the holy family fleeing in the darkness.

Back to the land of Egypt we were going. Back to the place where Moses delivered the people of Israel so long ago.

Mary hugged him, then Ruth, then Simon, and finally Levi.

Zebby knelt and Joe helped Mary onto his saddle then reached into the casket of gold. "Here." He handed several pieces to Jacob.

"Everything was already provided. Glory to the Lord." Ruth raised her hands in a very solemn praise. "And may God guide and protect us all."

We all vacated the stable simultaneously. Nazareth on the one hand, Egypt on the other. Perhaps it would be one of the quickest journeys I had ever made, but getting back on the road to a foreign land? Oh, I had been prepared for *this*! I was ready to go once more. And this time, my burden was easy, my yoke (if I had worn one) was light. For love was my reason and I would take this family wherever The Most High led.

Joe mounted. "Let's go. We'll try and make it to Hebron today. Elizabeth and Zechariah will take us in for the night."

"Issy," Heffy said. "What will happen to me?"

Oh, my friend! "You will be taken by the relatives. You will be safe."

"Will I ever see you again?"

Donkeys have a hard time lying, even to make others feel better. "I don't know. The truth is, I'm not sure what's to become of me. But I do know that Jesus will grow up. Perhaps we can take comfort from that."

"I'll try."

Meanwhile, Jesus slept.

We were only a few miles down the road when the wind delivered to us the true intent of Herod in the cries of infants and their parents. A great wail bounced from hillside to hillside.

The house and the stable were searched by indiscriminate soldiers who were told but one thing: Kill them all. Kill every last male under the age of three.

There. Nice and tidy. My will be done.

Herod.

She did not weep in vain.

Chapter Seventeen

Zebby and I walked side by side for a brief respite from running, starlight and moonlight on the snaking path before us, the terrain of the Judean hills desolate.

"I can only picture what's going on back there," he said, when the daylight began gathering itself below the horizon. The stars just started to fade, the tiny lights so small to us, so great in reality, receding above the first light of dawn, though barely.

"We should have warned the others," I said to Zebby. "Why didn't anyone think to warn the others?"

The blood flowed, the blood of children. Parents, grandparents, brothers, sisters, aunts, uncles, cousins and friends, weeping.

Mary's voice echoed my thoughts. "Why us? I mean, I know why. This child, this baby that sleeps. Yes. But why do we get to live, why does Jesus, and they don't? Little ones, precious in the eyes of God, are dying today. And mothers just like me weep, wail, and the mourning will begin, such as never before been heard in Bethlehem."

No angel for them. No dream. Just awakening to a nightmare, an utter nightmare. There's never a good time for anything like this. Trust me.

Joe's mouth set in a firm line. "Mary, I can't

stop thinking about it either. All I know is, we're doing what we were told. Listening to the angel. Getting our son out of there. But my heart is heavy. I feel no sense of joy in this, and my relief is only standing on the foundation of obedience. Nothing more."

"Perhaps God will stem the tide of Herod's wrath."

"This we cannot know."

"May they sleep in the arms of Adonai tonight," she whispered.

Oh, they will, Mary. They surely will.

I have seen my fair share of death in all my years. And it never seems to get easier, even though every being is precious to God. Every life. Every breath. Every death. And though they travel back to the arms of The Most High who made us, losing that piece of God's creation to this world never seems easy to humans.

"Our times are in God's hands, Issy," said Zebby. "Knowing that makes the difference somehow."

"God is merciful."

And yet, I am still bowed down with sorrow right now.

We sped up once more.

Around nine in the morning a cloud of dust kicked up on the road far behind us. Joe noticed.

"Horses," he said to Mary. "They're traveling fast."

I felt it. Zebby did too.

Danger.

"Mary, hold on and continue toward Hebron. If you can't make it to Elizabeth's and need to rest, find a safe place among the hills. I have no doubt that if I can't find you, Issy surely will."

Yes, that is true!

"Oh, I can track, too," said Zebby.

"Yes, but you'll already be there, Zebby."

"If we veer off the path, I will drag a foot in that direction and pray the wind doesn't cover it over, Starlight."

We had a plan.

Mary secured Jesus to her with a length of cloth. Now awake, he looked all around pointing out rocks and trees and birds. Joe tucked his son's head into the binding to secure his neck. "Son, if you stay still right now, so much the better for you and your mother."

"What if—" Mary began.

"No what ifs, my love. I will see you much sooner than you think. We may do well to bed down for the day anyway and resume our trek after moonrise tonight." He gave an easy swat to Zebby's backside. "Now run, Zebby! Run!"

And Zebby ran! Stretching his long neck into the future, he sped on skinny legs as his feet pummelled the ground.

The dust cloud behind us grew closer.

"We don't have much time now, Issy." Joe mounted my back. "I know you have it in you. But just in case, be ready to make a run for it if we have to. With your sure feet, we can lose them in the hills."

Fourteen hundred years of strength, service, and loyalty shot through my heart and into my veins. The Most High would mount us up on wings as eagles if that was needed. Peace settled onto me.

We rode along faster than we ever had, Joe and me, but I didn't mind. It was good to stretch my legs and push the boundaries for a bit. This old gal still had it in her. I would do all I could to protect my family. The wind blew at our backs, God be thanked, and I ran like an arrow.

But as fast as I went, Zebby left us behind with ease.

"That is some camel," Joe said.

Indeed.

"Can you go even faster?"

I couldn't. I tried, but soon my lungs began to labor, and I wondered if my legs would fail me eventually. If I had been a hundred years younger . . .

Joe leaned over. "It's okay, girl. Don't endanger yourself. God will take care of us."

I let up just a bit.

He looked over his shoulder. "They're gaining on us! Perhaps we can detain them by a long conversation of where we are going, what for, and why. It should buy Zebby, Mary, and Jesus more time. Let's take a break."

Joe slipped down, gave me water and a handful of grain, bless him.

He took my reins and we walked along like any simple man and his donkey. They really could have been anybody, the people behind us. Bandits, of course. Herod's men, messengers, people fleeing for their own particular needs. Romans. There were so many reasons for haste we could assume none of them.

Joe covered his head with his mantle and continued steadily on, brave. "Zebby will outrun them if he hasn't done so already."

We rounded curves knowing the group gained on us. When appropriate, Joe turned and hailed them.

They advanced and finally slowed and stopped beside us. Roman soldiers and one fellow in chains. Prisoner transport, probably messages too. Who could know with Romans? They knew better than most how to hide in plain sight. When you're that powerful, you have to.

Joe shielded his eyes to look up at the soldier in command as he said, "And what bade you be in such a hurry back there?"

"My donkey likes to do things her way."

Joe was right about that. All donkeys do. It's just that we hardly ever get the opportunity.

"I find if I let her have her way for part of the day, she's much more willing to do what I ask for the rest of it."

This was very true. Only treats were usually a part.

The soldier laughed. "Sounds like a lot of women I know!"

What cheek!

"Where are you headed?"

"Alexandria." He patted his tool kit. "I am a tekton. There's good work there right now."

"There's a good community of Jews there. Quite large," he said.

Oh, what a beautiful horse he rode! Large and white. A stallion.

"Festus," the horse said. "Hello, Starlight."

"You know me?"

"Yes. Whatever you're up to, it's safe with me. The beasts have heard tell you're on the mission of your life these days. God speed."

"Be careful," the soldier advised. "This isn't a safe road."

"Thank you," said Joe. "We'll do our best."

"Nice donkey you've got there. A little rough around the edges but she's got a nice healthy sparkle in those eyes."

A nice healthy sparkle? I'll take it.

And off they rode.

Joe mounted me once more, relief permeating his body. "Let's pick up the pace a little now, Issy. Stay in their wake a bit, for safety's sake."

And all the sooner to get back to my Mary.

"The truth is, Rome will not come to Herod's aid with this. They have bigger problems than a madman's whims."

And so I ran. Not at full speed, but enough to reunite this family once again. We would cross the border soon enough.

"Alexandria," whispered Joe. "Yes. Yes. That is where we will go."

We ran for a while, and I saw it, the dragging mark of Zebby's hoof.

I slowed down and stopped.

"Issy! Now's not the time for you to become stubborn."

But I wouldn't move. And the good thing about this situation was that I knew Joe wouldn't treat me harshly and beat me in the way that rascal Balaam did.

"I don't know what you're up to Issy, but I've been around you enough to know you're right about these things."

Isn't Joe the best?

He did not join us in vain.

Chapter Eighteen

We began circumnavigating the hillside. Fifteen minutes into the trek Joe pointed his finger and cried, "Look, Issy!"

A cloud, small and white, hovered like a lamb above an outcropping of rock.

"Could that be . . ." Joe shielded his eyes. "No. Wait a moment." He bent forward at the waist then turned to me. "Issy, do you see that?"

I squeaked.

"A cloud by day."

And it was. Not only did Zebby mark the beginning of the trail, he gave us markings along the way. Here a dragged hoofmark, there a giant wad of spit that was almost dry but enough for me to notice.

There tucked between two great boulders sat Mary, Jesus, and Zebby. Although Zebby was standing guard.

"Joe!" she cried, scooping Jesus into her arms. "You found us!"

"Look up, Mary!" He pointed to the cloud that had not only provided direction but had given his family shade as well.

She laughed. Jesus clapped his hands. "Issy!" he cried, leaning so far forward Mary had to catch him.

"I have to tell you, though, before we saw the cloud,

Issy refused to go further. She somehow knew you were over here. She weaved a good bit once we were off the path. I don't know what that was about."

Joe led me to stand next to Zebby as he walked back into the roomy crevice with his wife and son.

"What happened, Mary?"

"It was all Zebby. Thank Adonai for that little camel. All of a sudden he veered left and made straight for this hiding spot. I set Jesus down and he wandered just over there." She pointed to a smaller crevice. "I watched him pat the rock in there, Joe. A spring bubbled up. It's small but we can refill our water skins."

Joe went over to look. "Mary! Like Moses, only patient."

"He brings forth living water at his touch alone."

We watched for signs of intruders while Joe bedded down for sleep in preparation for the coming night. Mary slept too. Jesus, on the other hand was wide awake but stayed within the confines. Thankfully, he would have to get past us to move into full view and I already decided my bray would sound the alarm if necessary. Sometimes a donkey needs to plan ahead.

"Good job, Zebby. My goodness you made the way plain. I did my best to cover up the tracks."

"I had no doubt you'd find us. And now there's this cloud. I wonder if everyone can see it?"

"I don't know." The road wasn't visible from our vantage point. "We should probably stick to the wilderness. If Jesus can summon water, we'll be all right."

"He's quite the child, isn't he?"

I shook off the dust of the road a little. "Yes, he is. I imagine the mysteries we'll see are just getting started."

"I could have been left in the care of much worse humans." Zebby's voice dropped.

"I'm sorry you had to leave your home, your family, your good master."

"At least I know why now. Caspar seems to know how to respond to the deeper things, the wordless requests. I just never thought it would be me." Sadness still tinted him. "The last thing he whispered to me was, 'Sometimes we must give to The Most High that which is most precious to us. And so I consign you to his service, my noble friend.' But I miss him, Starlight."

"I know how that is. At least with me, I knew that none of my families and people would outlive me. Before now, anyway.”

“Yes. You do know. You’ve lost many that you’ve loved, haven’t you?”

My head bowed. “It hurts too much to think about it most days. And now I have Mary and Joe. And Jesus, too. They’re enough. Not because they have to be, but because I said *yes* to that.”

“Wise words, my friend.”

“Yes just means yes right now. And right now, here we are. We have a job to do, people to love, and we are valued. And The Most High sees us, Zebby. Never forget that.”

“I try not to.”

“I’m glad you’re with us. I know you’d rather be with your master, but maybe you’ll come to love us enough to give your heart some comfort.”

“Sleep a little, Starlight,” said Zebby. “We’ve been here for some time. I will take the first watch.”

“You don’t have to tell me twice, friend. And I thank you.”

I tucked my legs beneath me, settling in. “And the name is Is, if you don’t mind.”

“Is it is,” he said. He lifted his fine head, regal and studied, and watched the horizon. “You know, I believe this is a great purpose for me. I was all set to buckle under my own sense of desperation. Being taken away from the only human one has ever loved is no small thing for a beast.”

“Not small at all. Humans think we have no feelings.”

Zebby snickered. “My heart still pains me, Is. But it is also filled with love. I felt the presence of that baby upon my back, a glorious shine that radiated through his mother and into me.”

“I know what you mean.”

“Caspar possessed a good shine, but nothing like this.”

I could feel the shine of Jesus from here. And so I slept.

When I awakened several hours later, Jesus sat next to me, upon a slab of rock, building a little house of stone upon its foundation. “Issy!” he said. “Look!”

I nuzzled him, and he nuzzled back.

Jesus speaks donkey.

Zebby put his head down near the child. They nuzzled too.

I realized something that day. Jesus knew the animals and loved them too. Jesus loved all the people and all the animals and everything God made.

Alexandria awaited. And someday, like Moses who sojourned in Midian before coming back to the place of his birth to deliver his people, Jesus would return to Israel.

And I would be with him, as The Most High wills, every step of the way.

"Zebby?"

"Yes, Is?"

"This may not be easy, but it will always be good because God is always good."

The little camel nodded. "I'm in. Every last inch of me. Inside and out."

A marvelous adventure was before us. For had not one been behind us too?

It's always a good time for an adventure with The Most High. I imagine Jesus will know that better than anyone. God made flesh. Here with us. *Never* to forget what it was like to be a human.

My dear friend, be sure to jot that down.

This is your helper. This is your deliverer. This is the One who loves you without fail.

And so we wandered in the wilderness, like Moses before us, returning to the very same Egypt from which Israel had come.

To be continued. . .

Thank You For Reading

To learn more about The Salish Sea Press and the *St.Is* series
visit us at https://salishsea.press/

Follow The Salish Sea Press on social media.
Facebook and Instagram: thesalishseapress

And don't forget about Old Is!
Instagram: asassysidekick

Other Titles by Leonard and Lisa

Author of over 60 books, Leonard Sweet's latest are:

Songs of Light series with Lisa Samson

St.Is with Lisa Samson

Contextual Intelligence with Michael Beck

Rings of Fire: Walking in Faith Through a Volcanic Future

Mother Tongue

The Bad Habits of Jesus

~ ~ ~ ~ ~

Author of over 40 books, Lisa Samson's reader favorites are:

We Had Stars in Our Eyes

Songs of Light series with Leonard Sweet

St.Is with Leonard Sweet

Quaker Summer

The Passion of Mary-Margaret

Embrace Me